My First 365 Coloring Book

This book belongs to

....

Wonder House

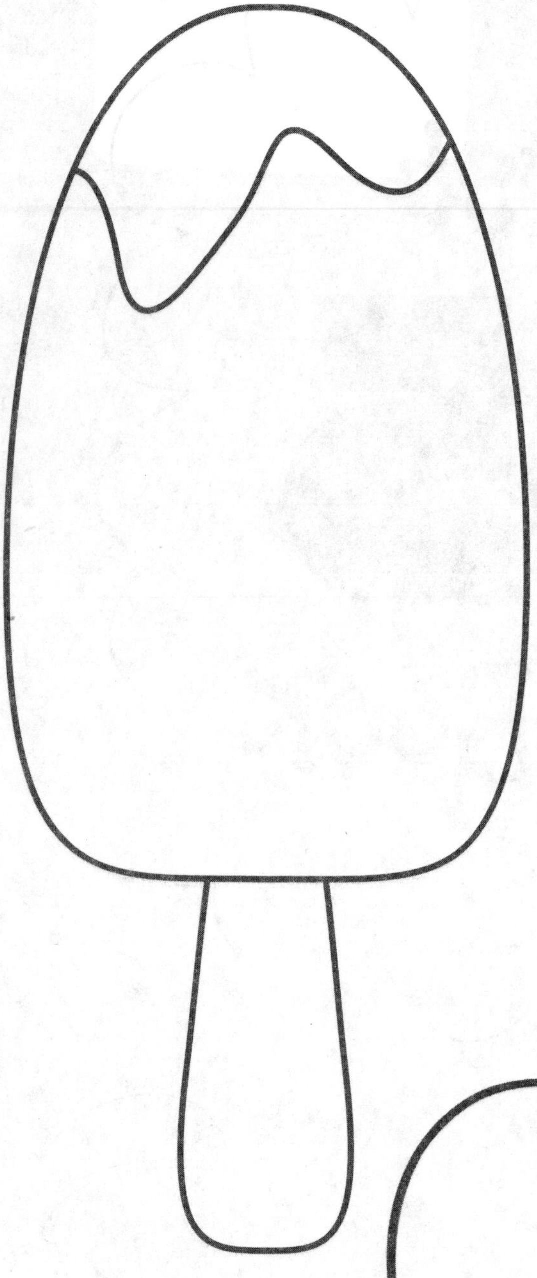

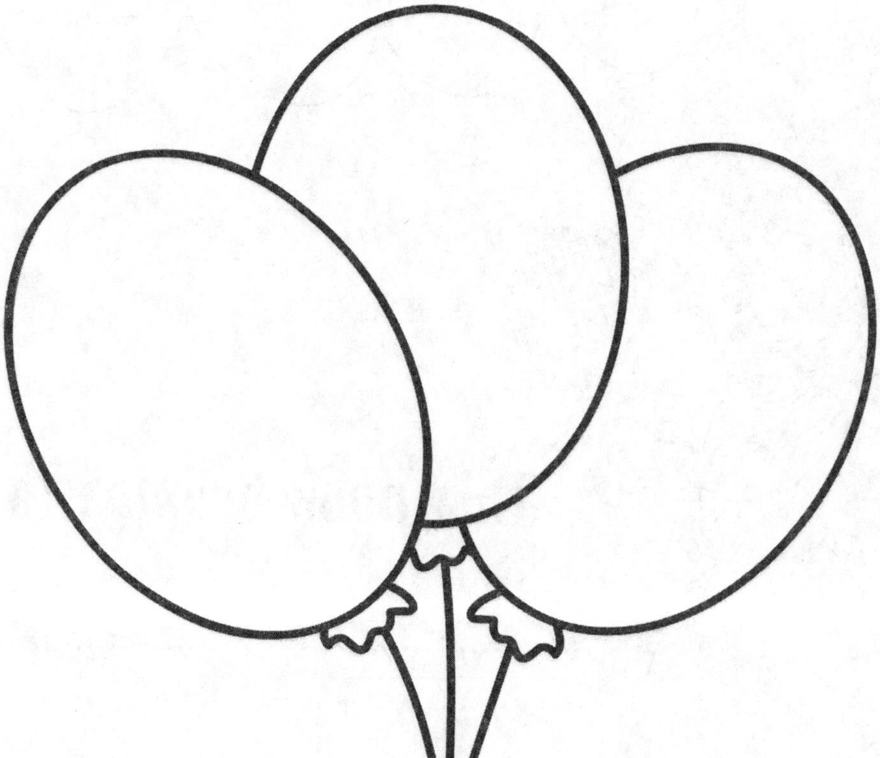

3

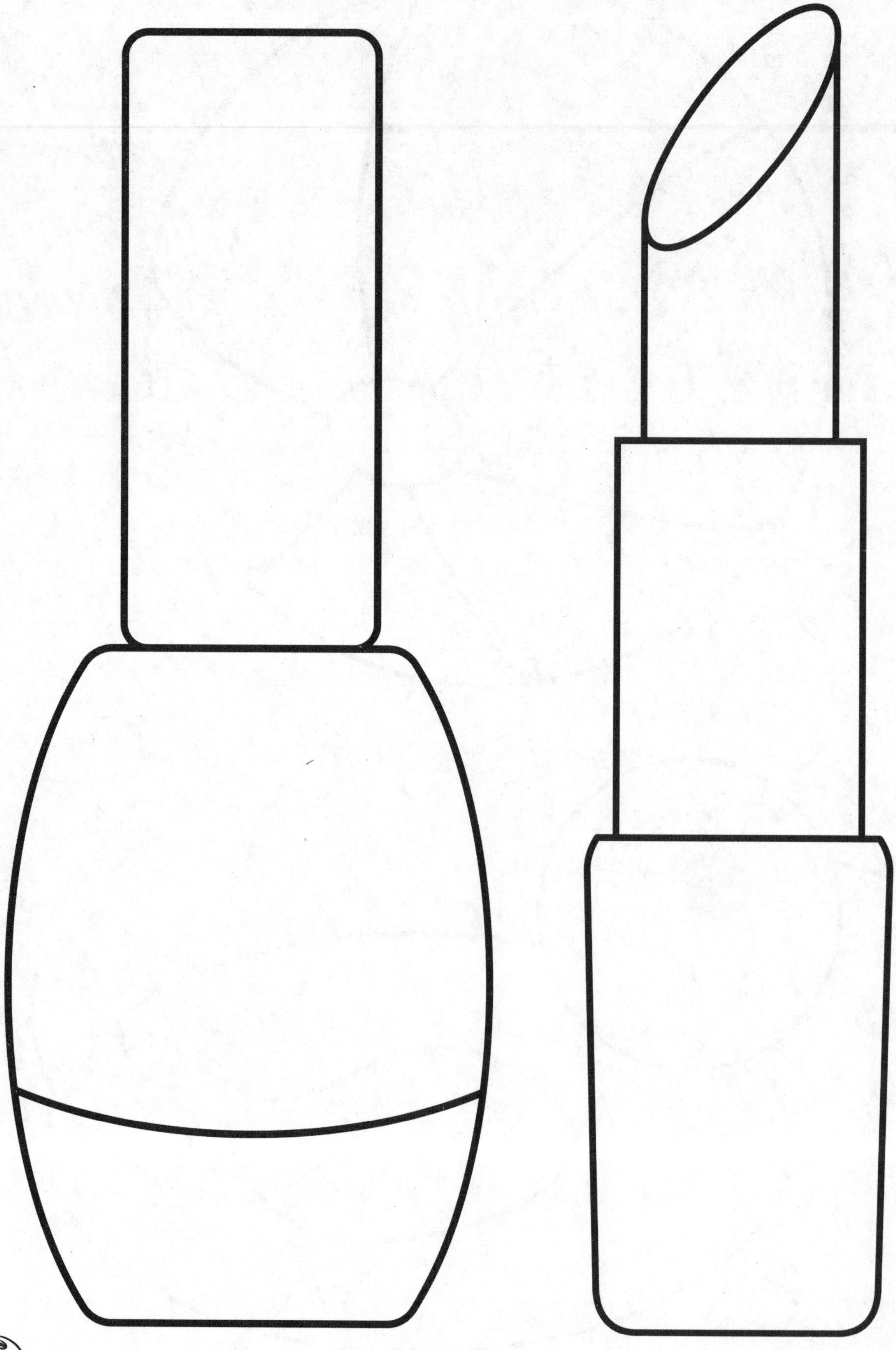

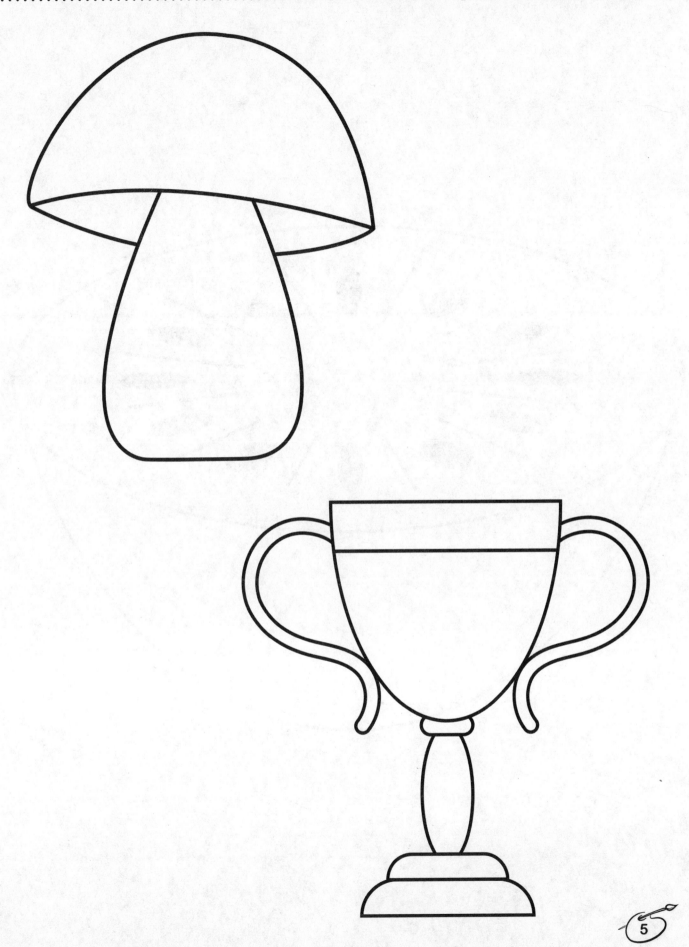

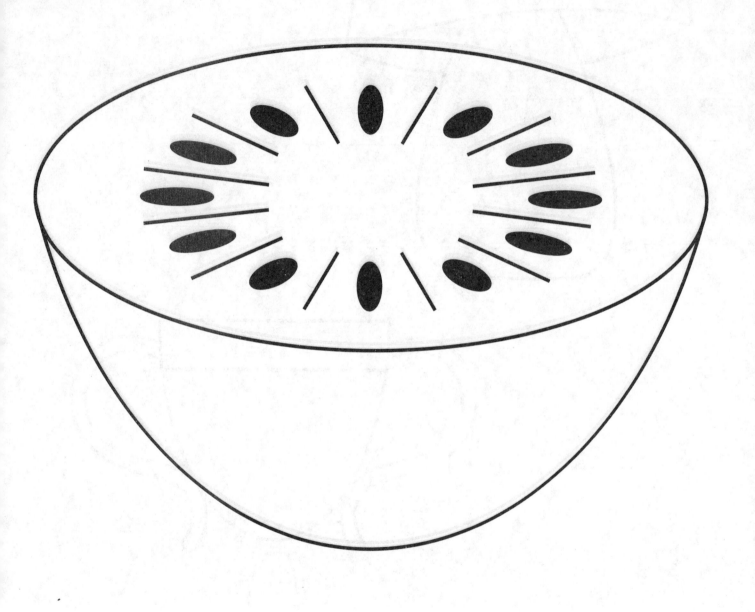

9

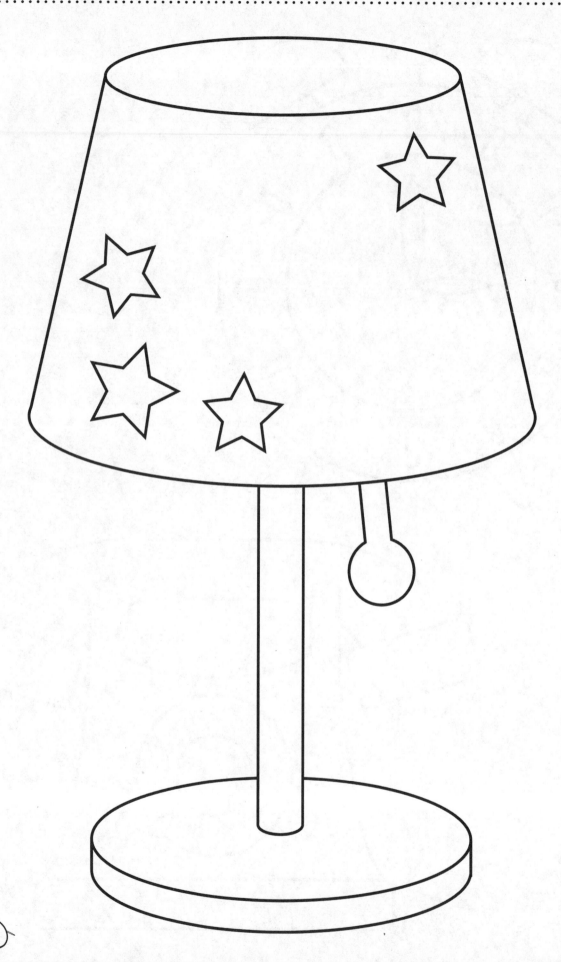

12

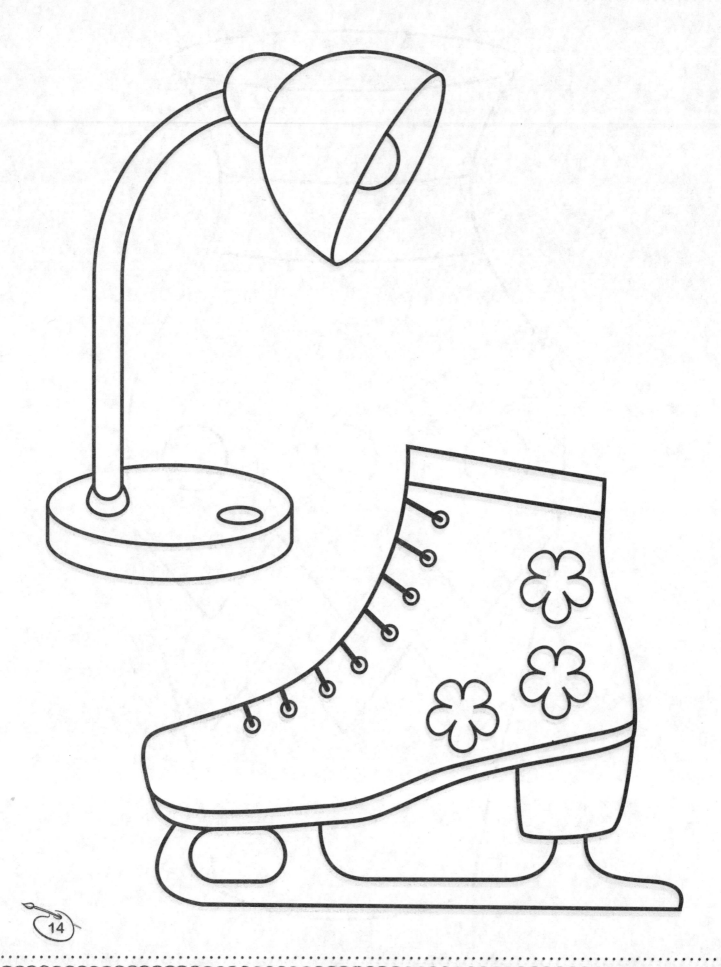

14

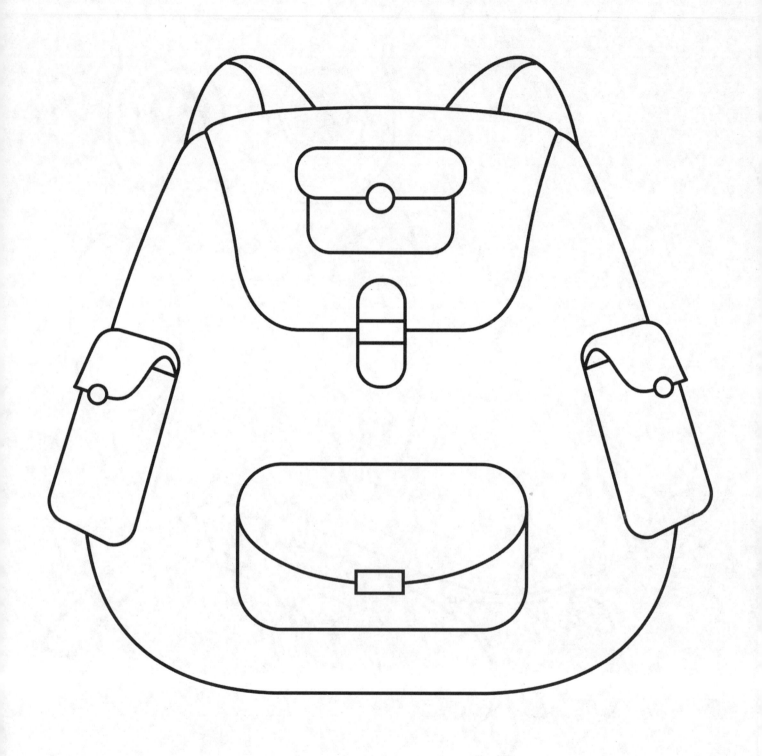

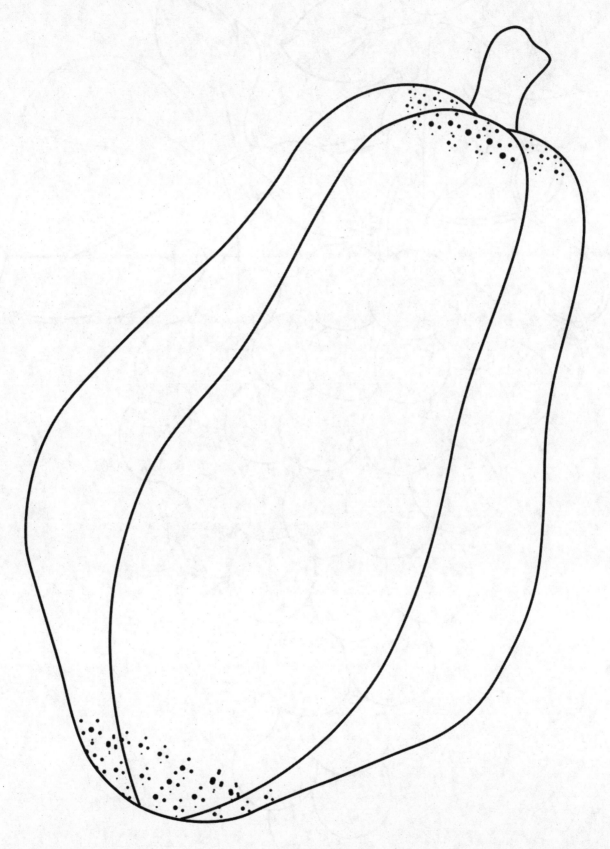

18

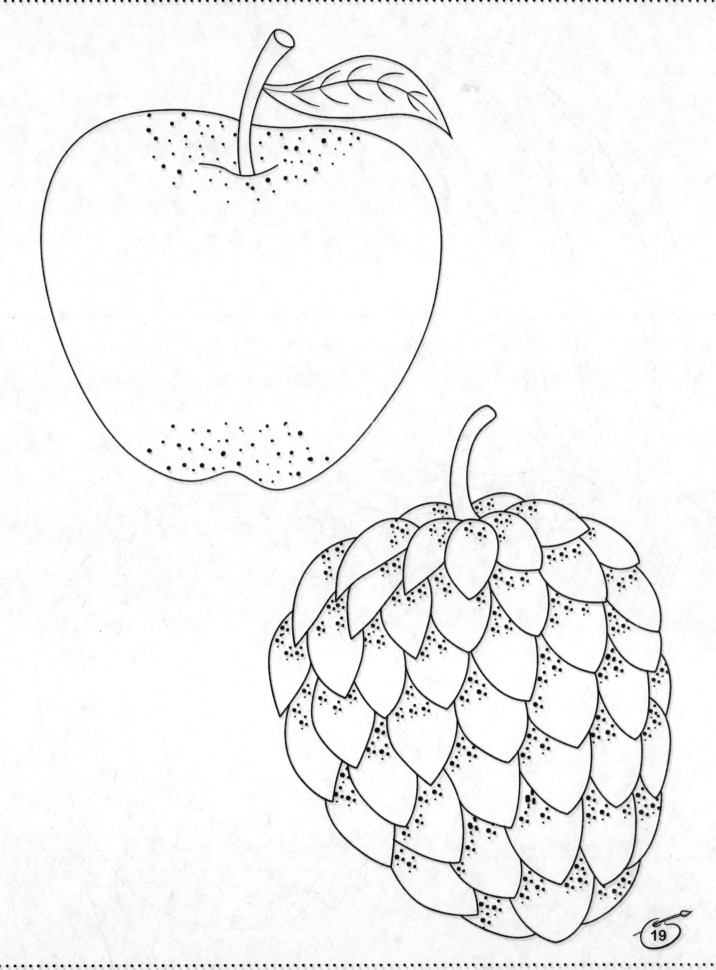

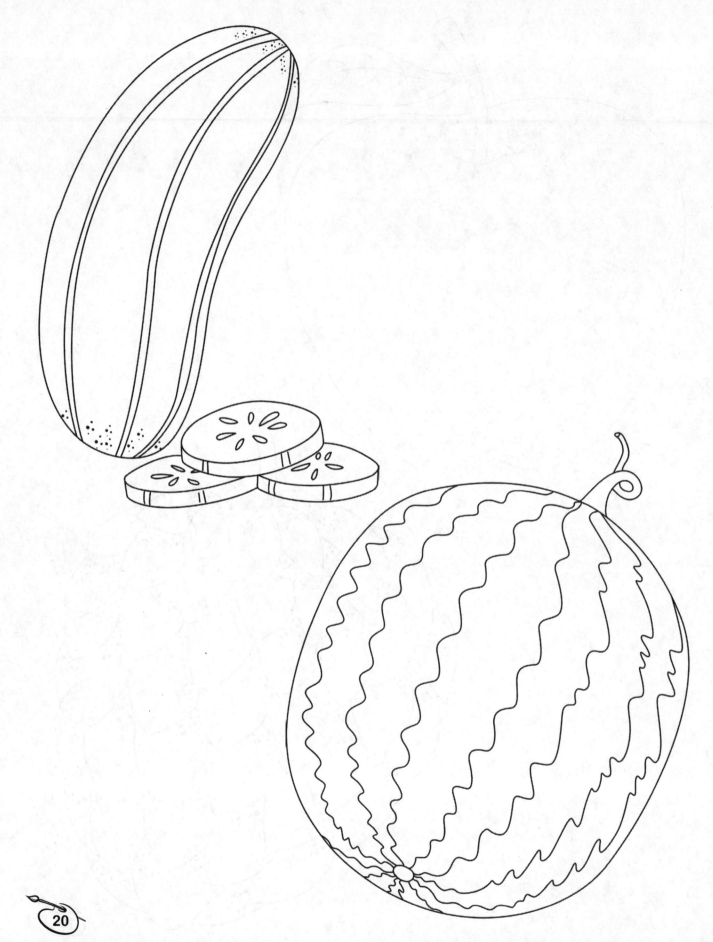

21

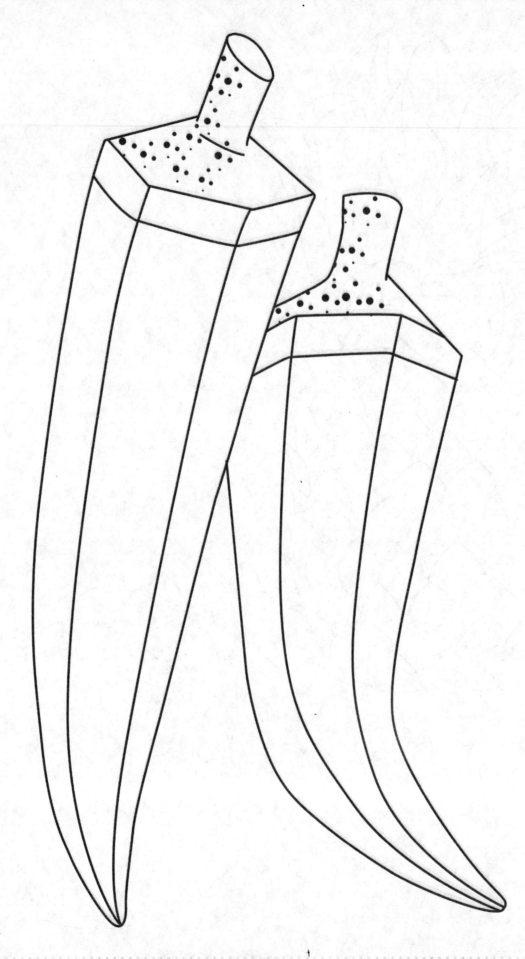

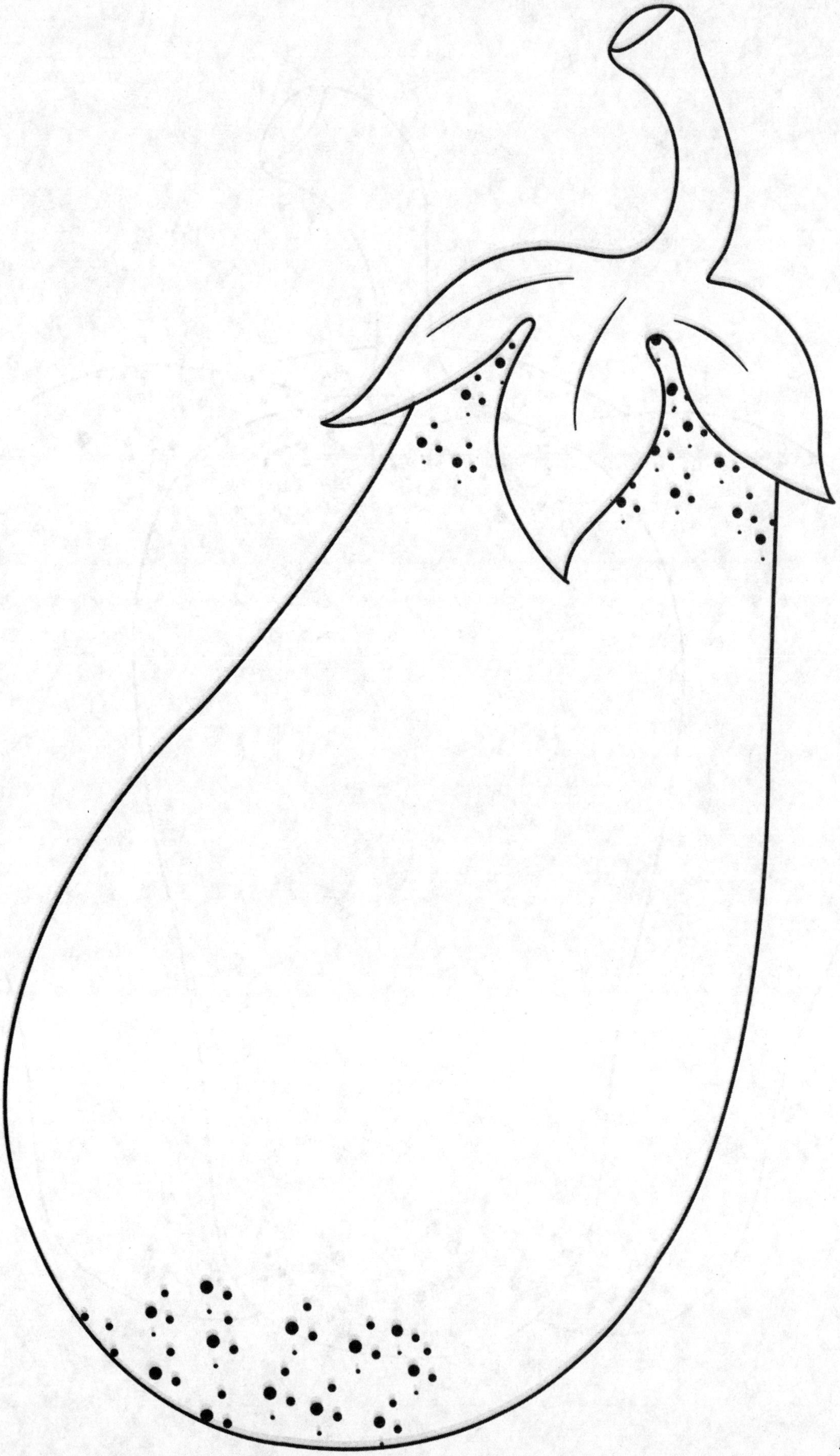

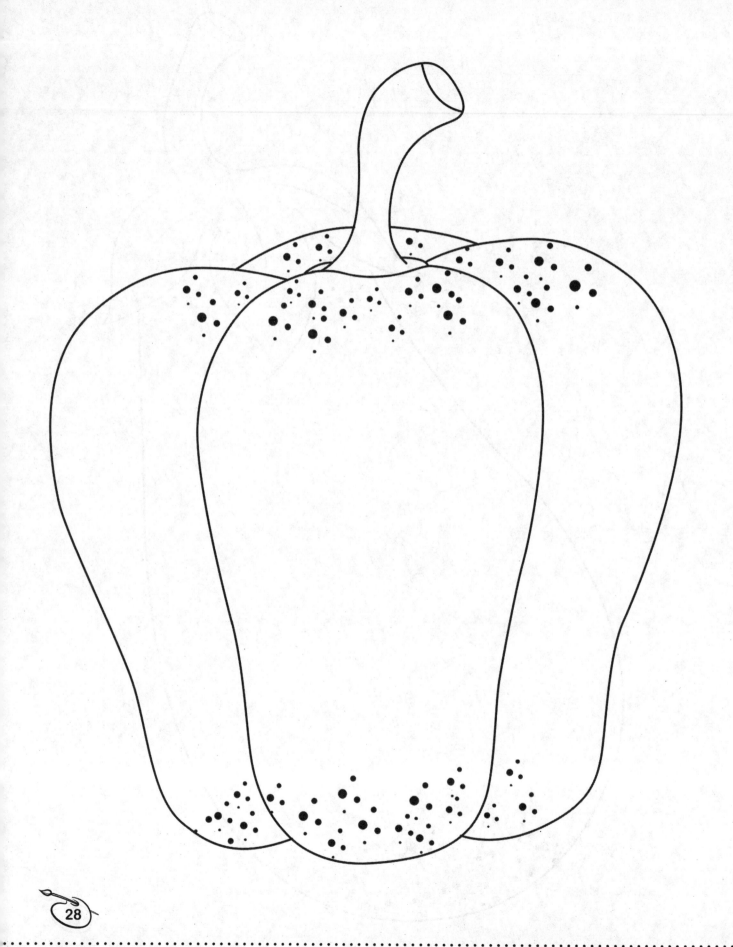

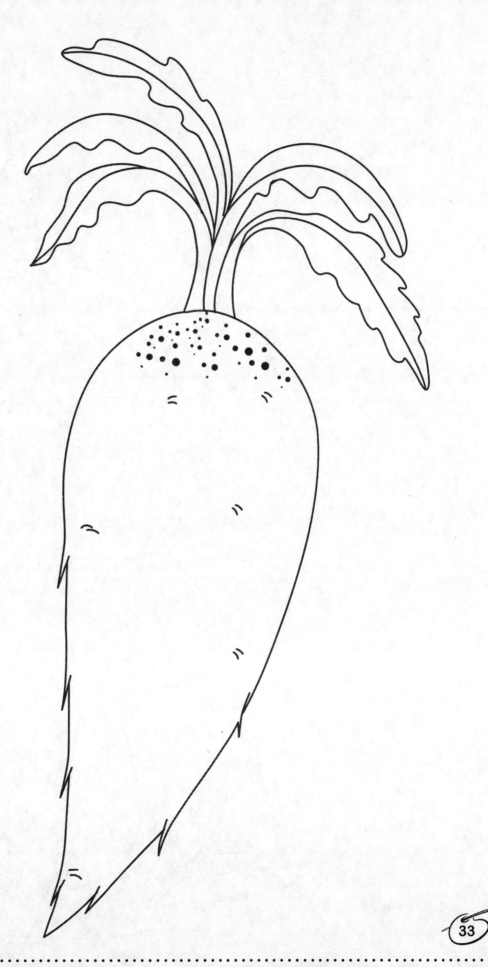

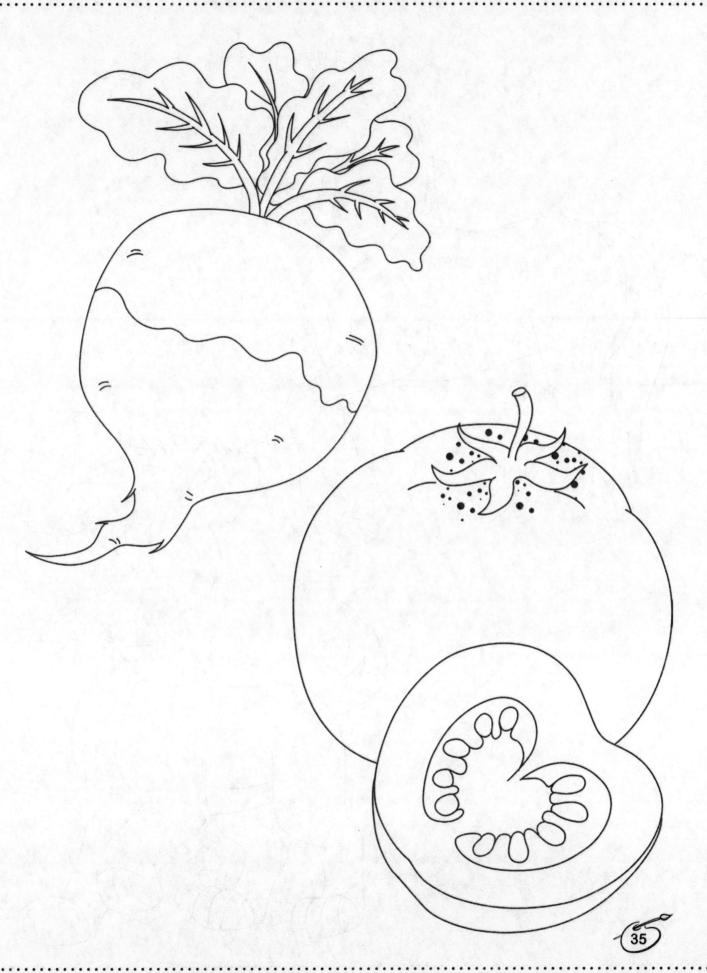

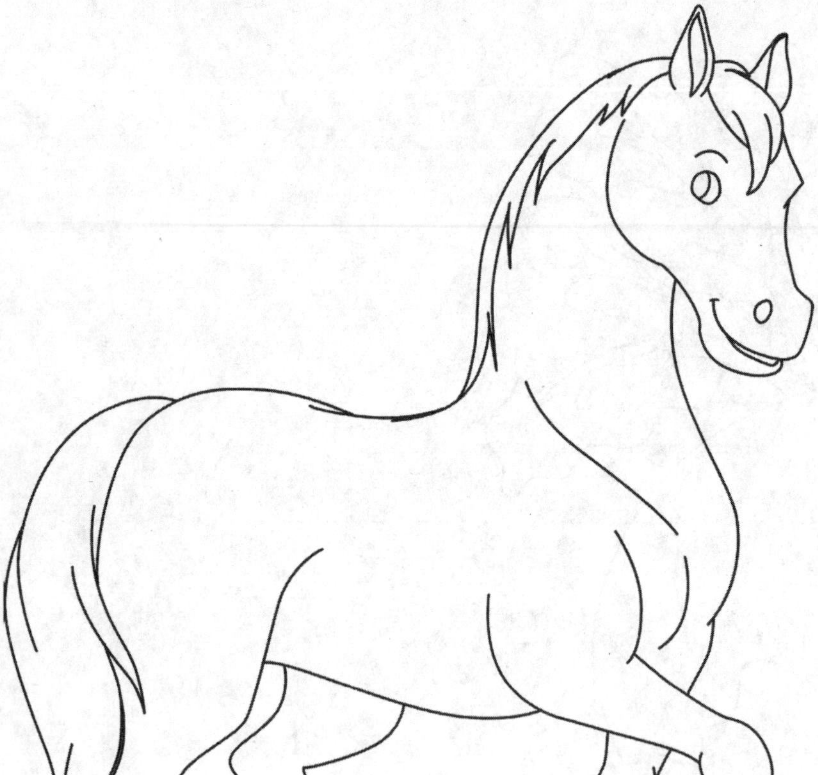

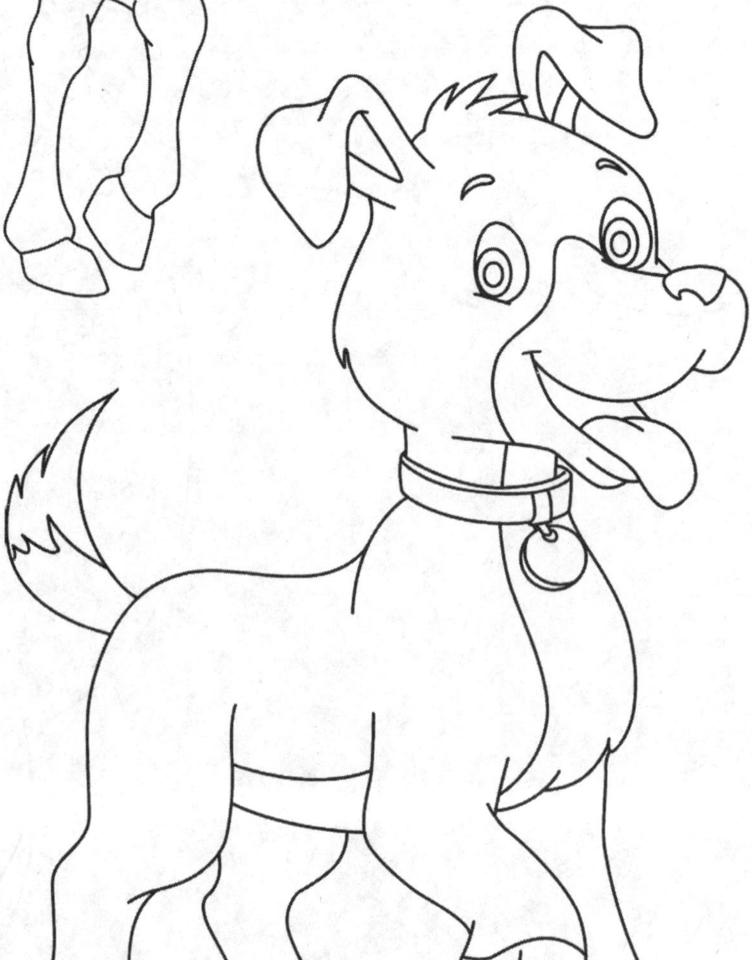

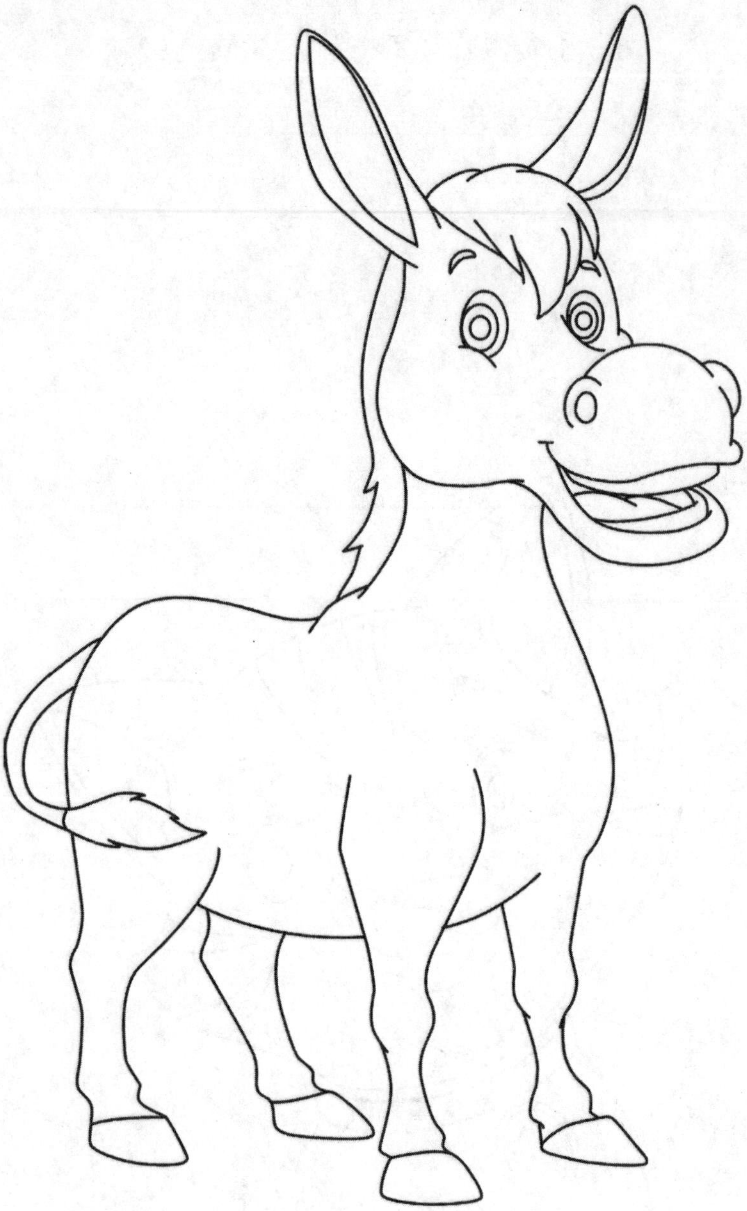

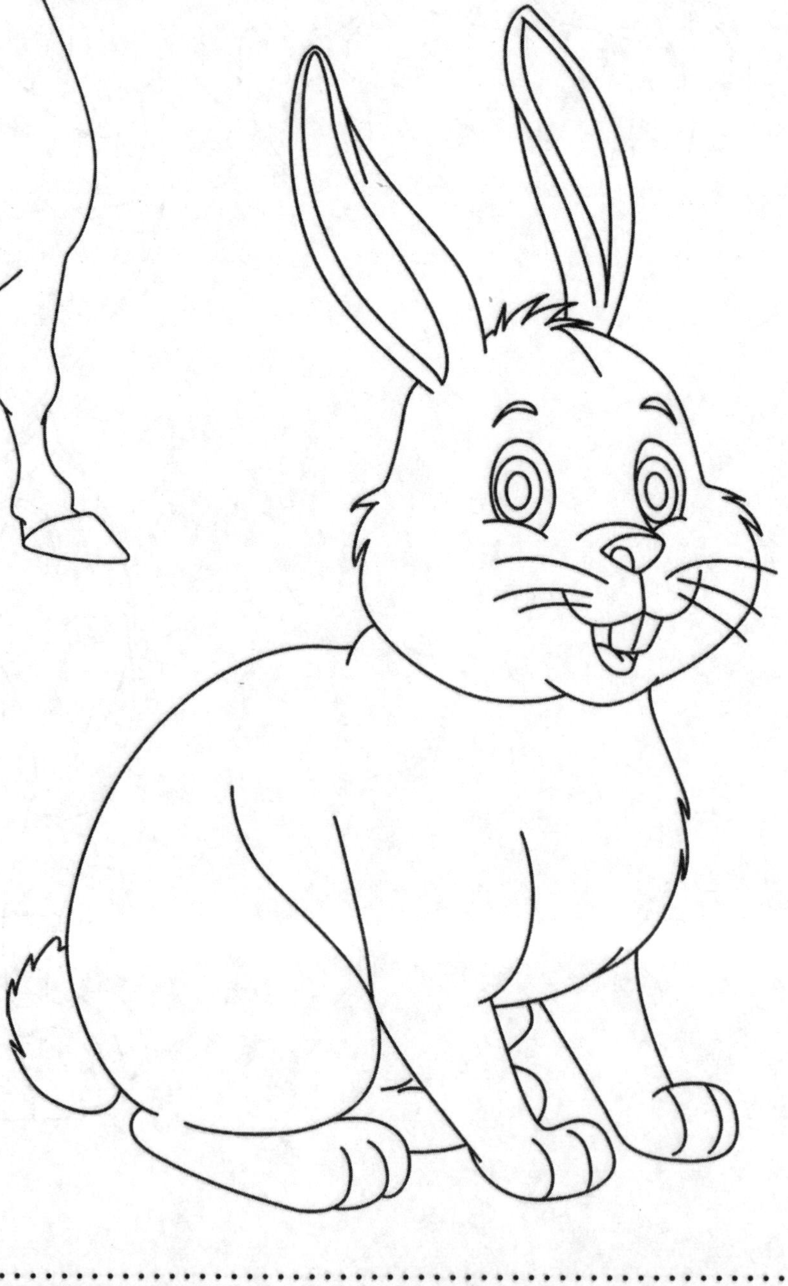

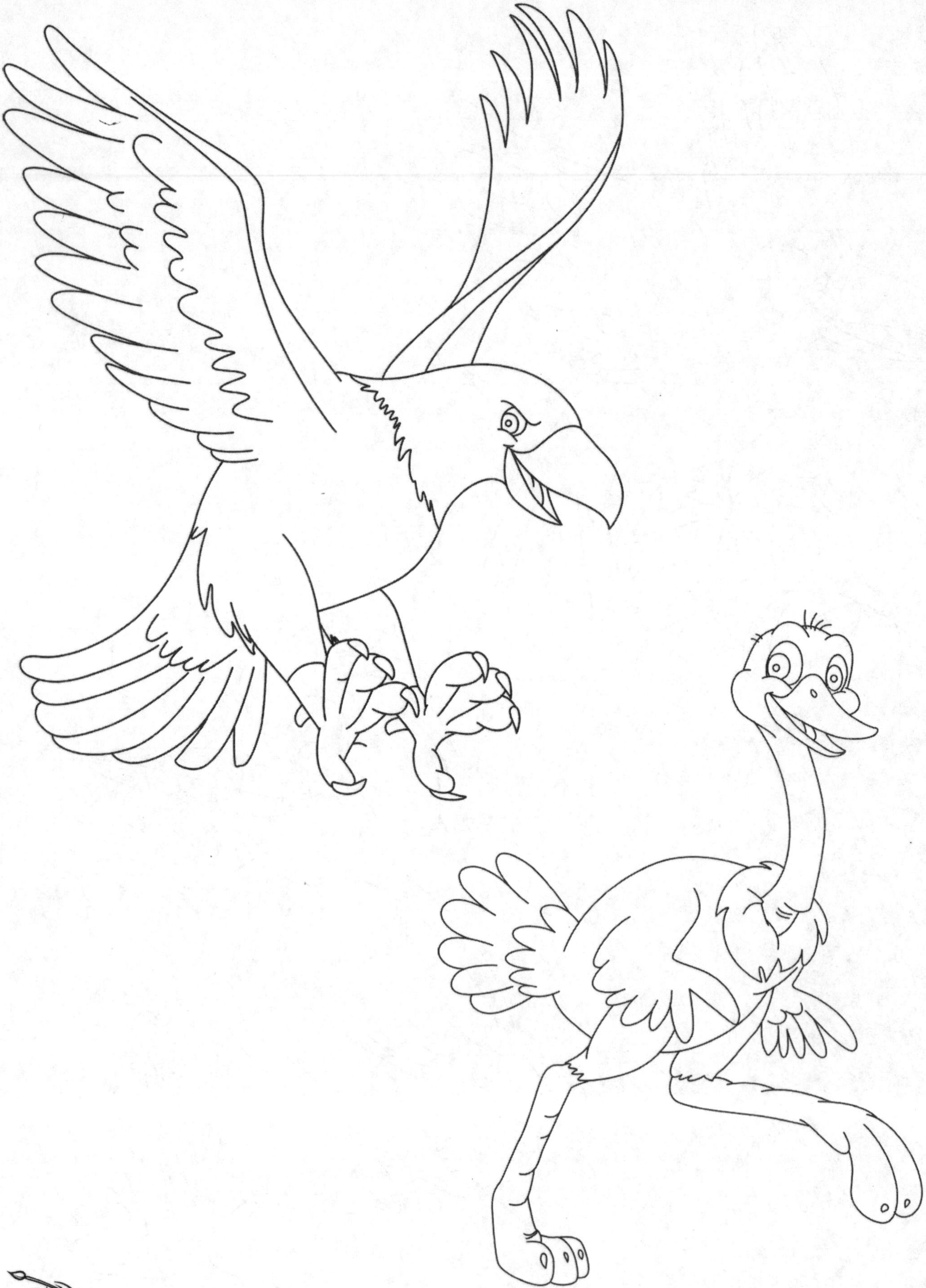

49

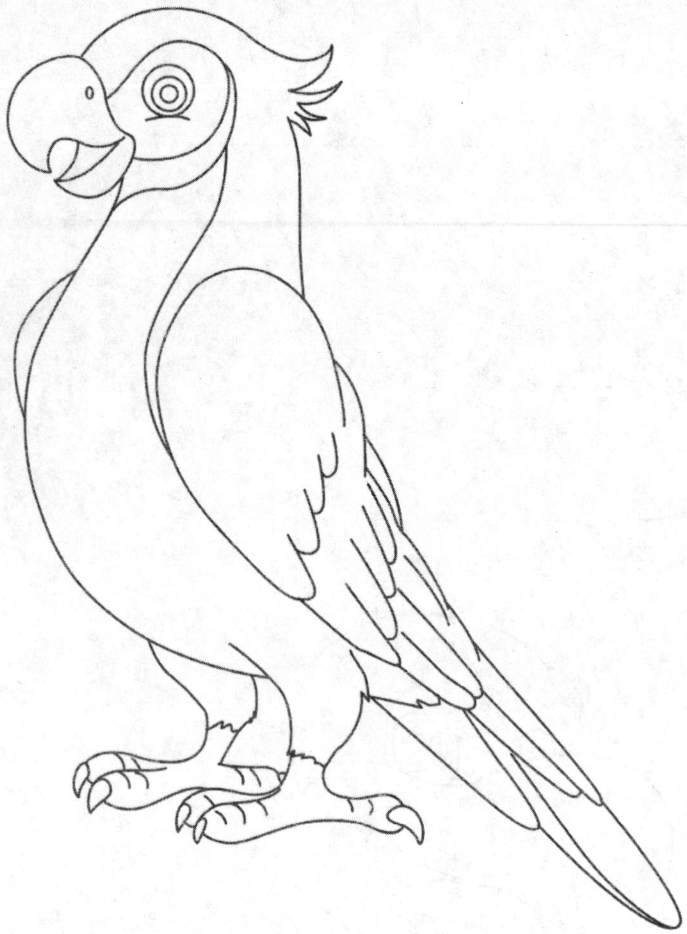

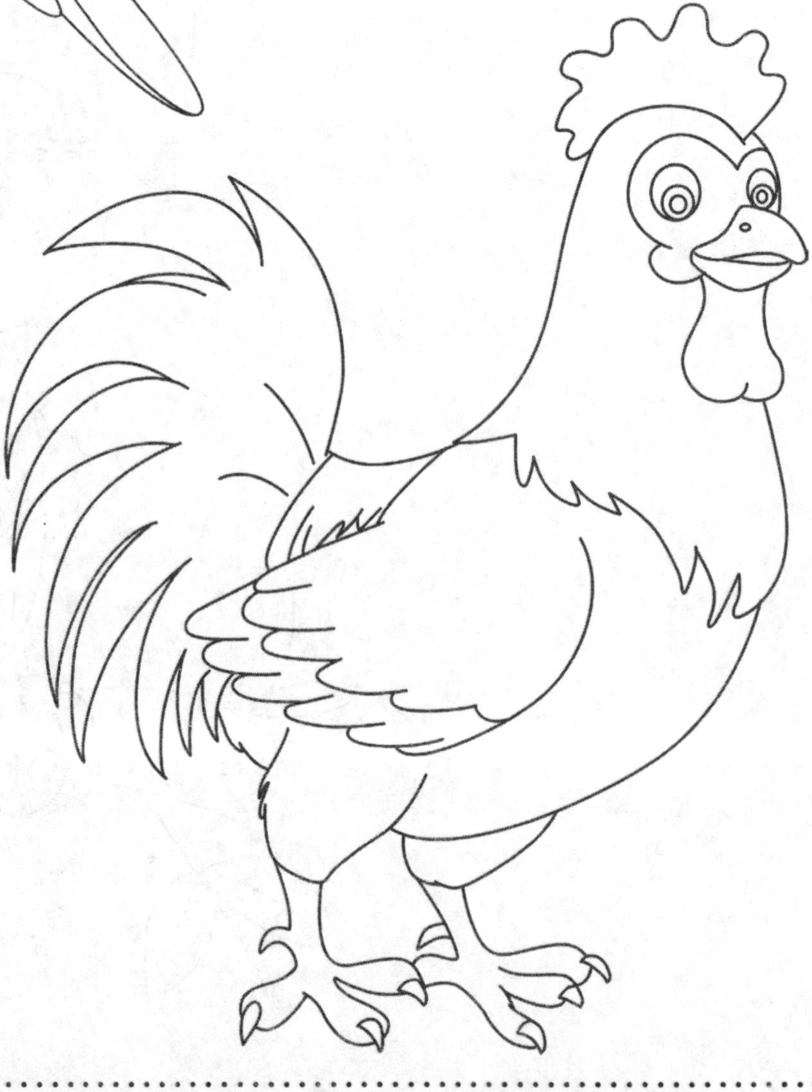

51

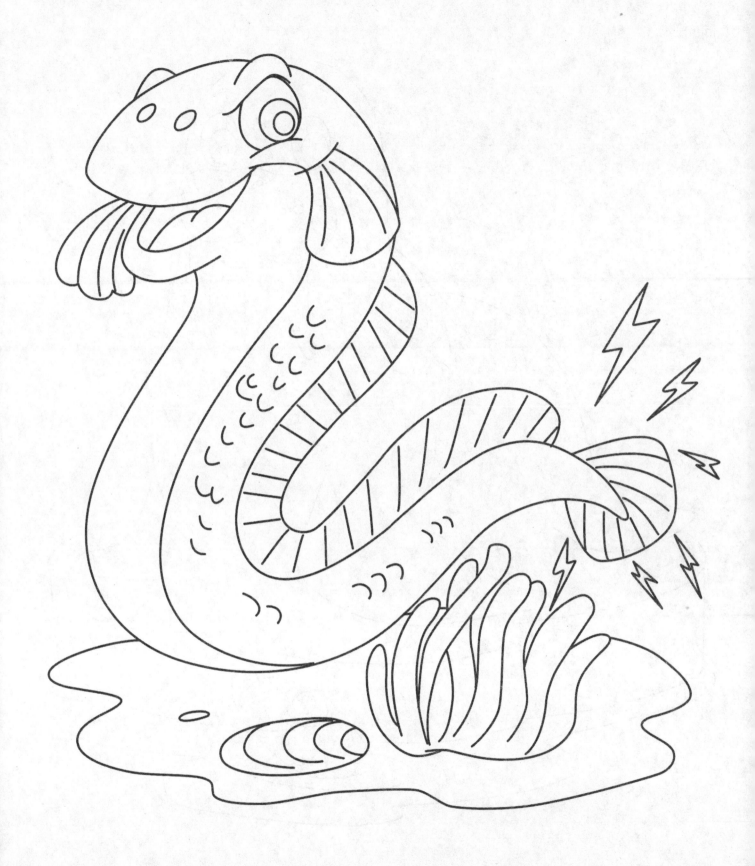

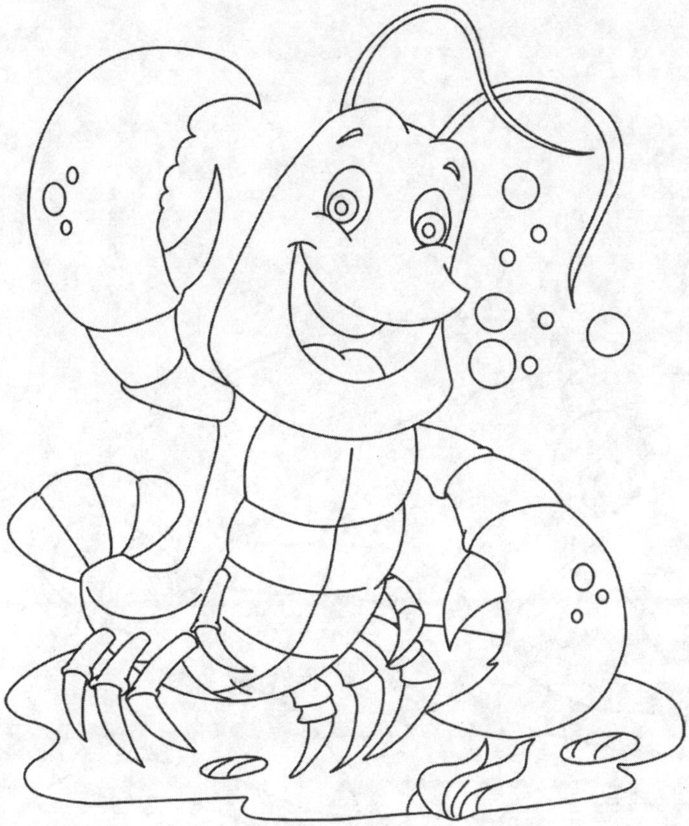

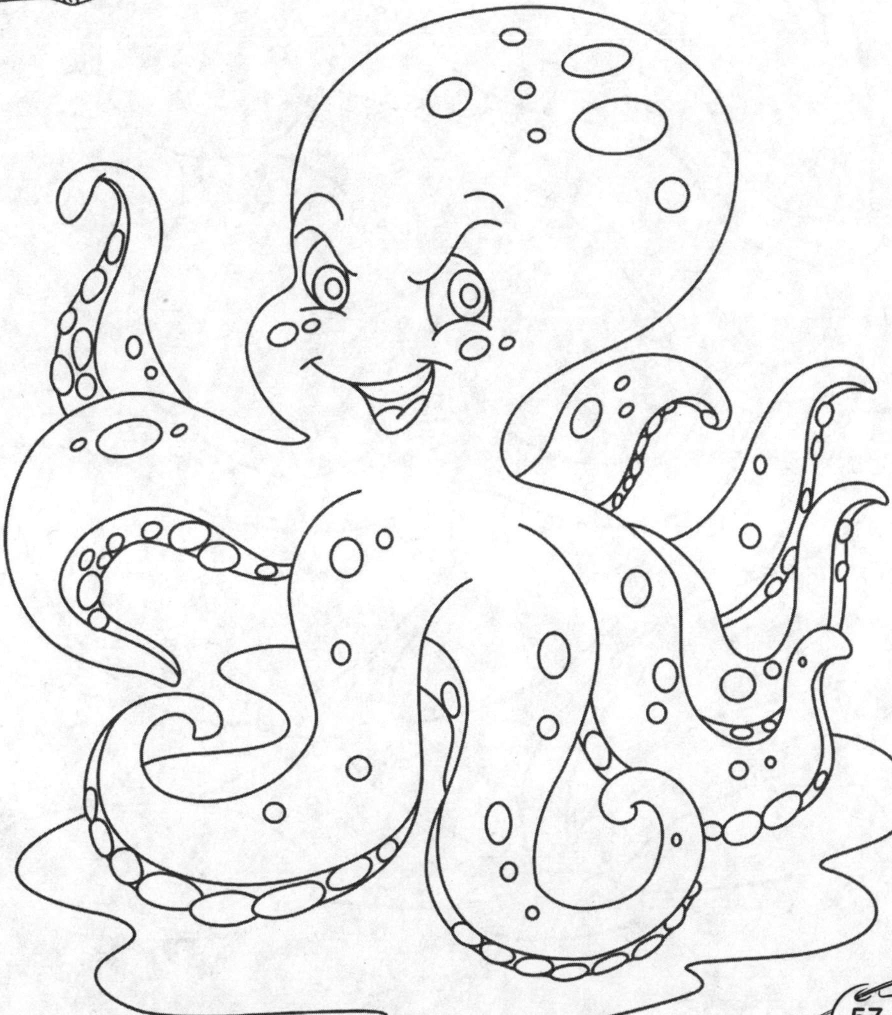

71

73

77

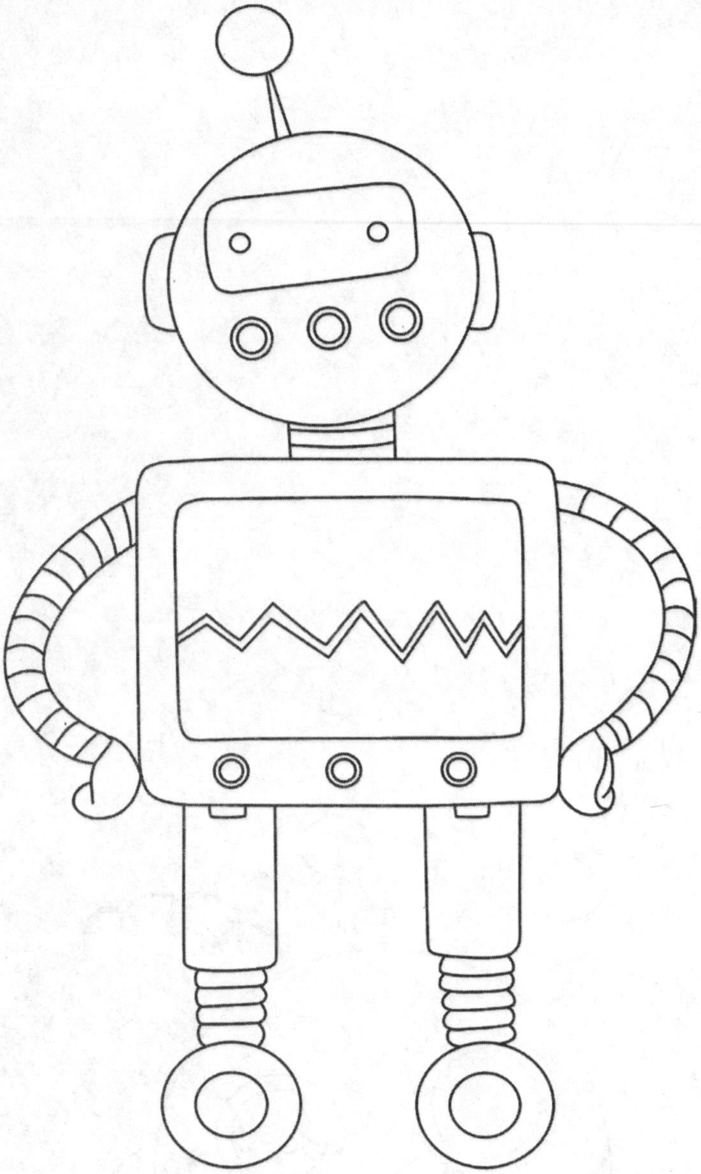

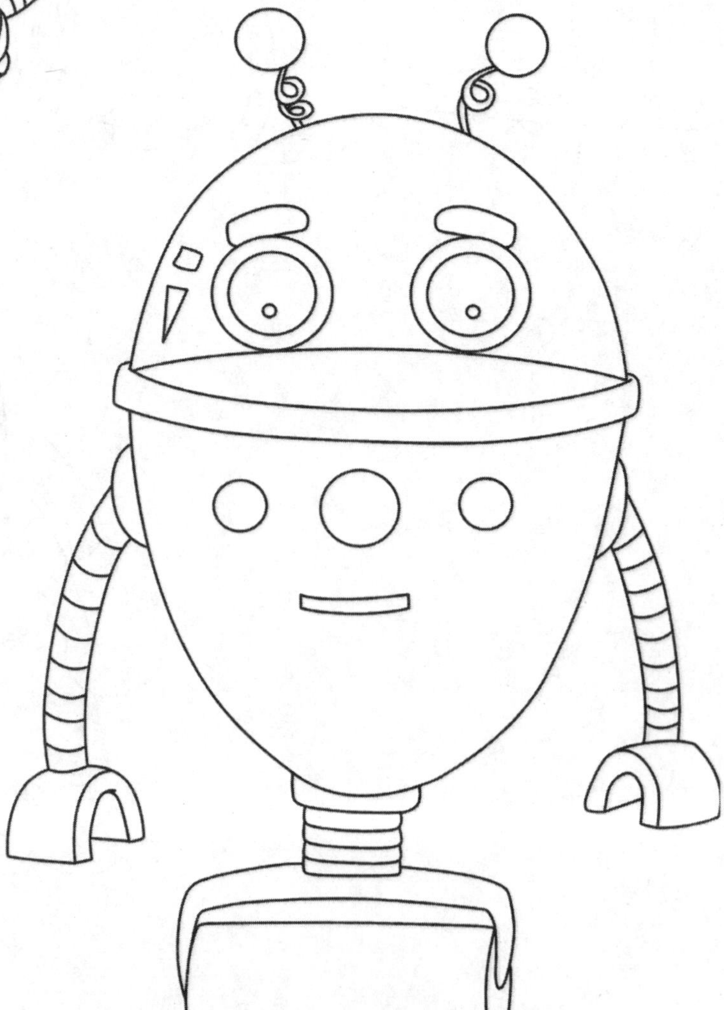

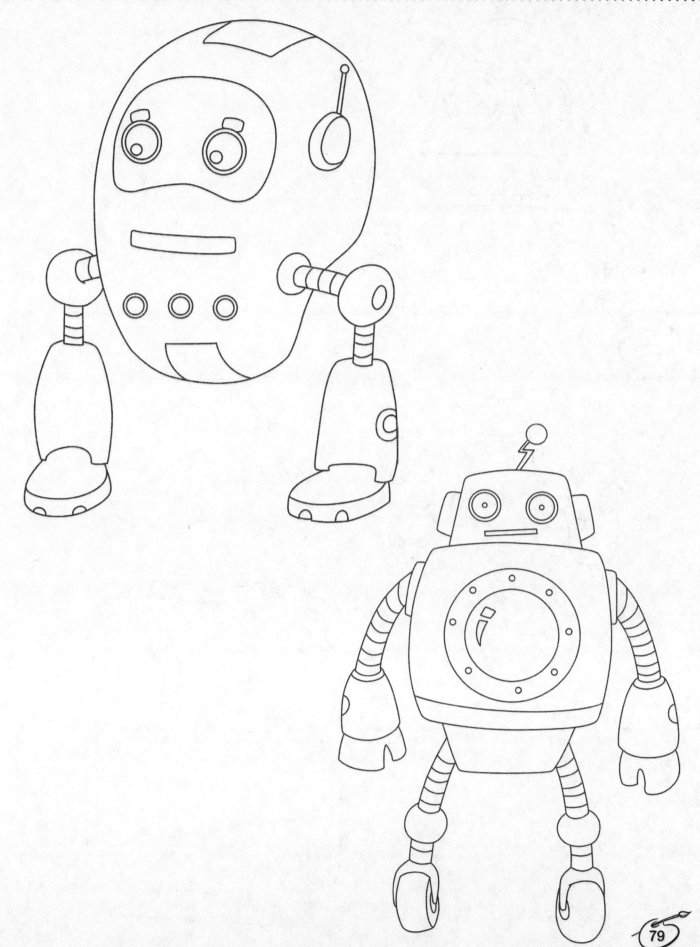

81

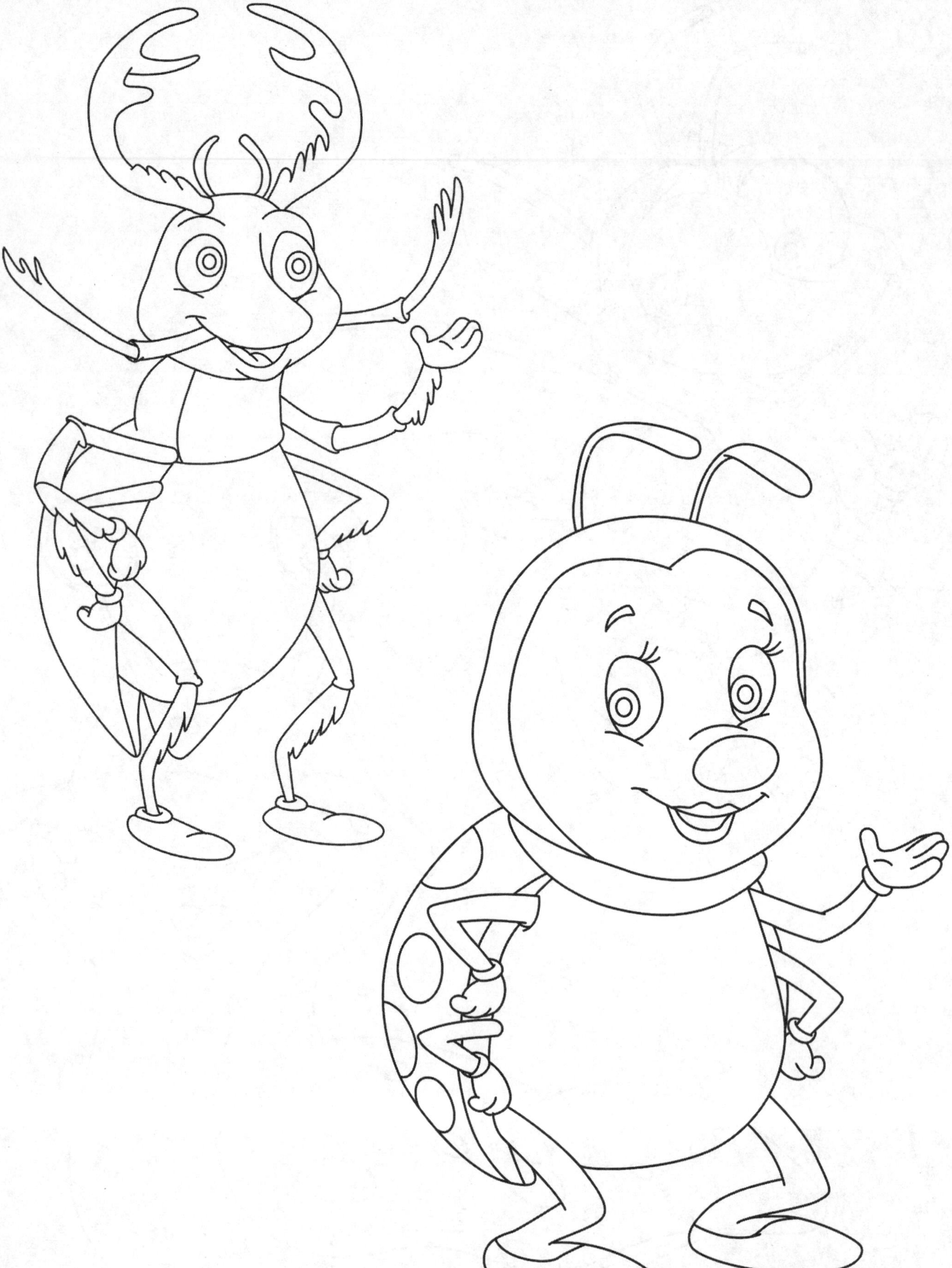

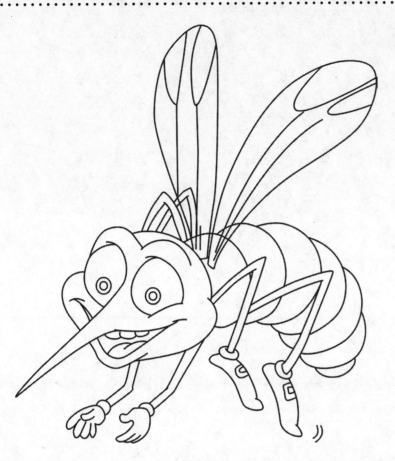

93

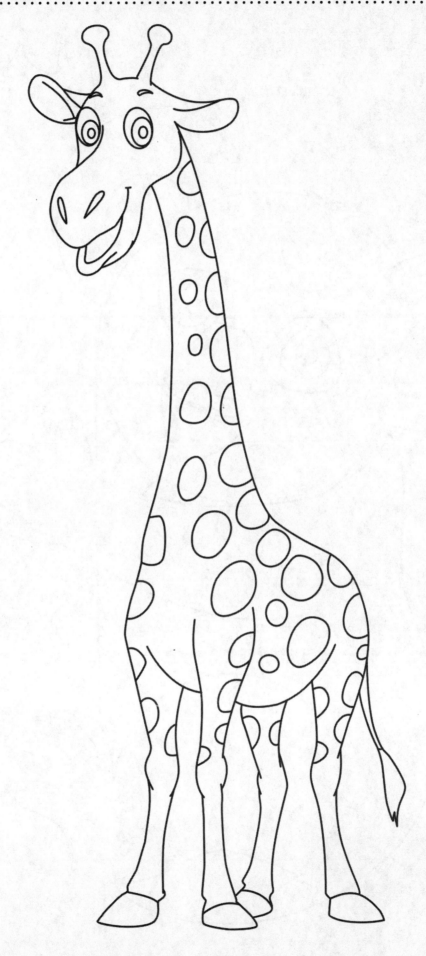

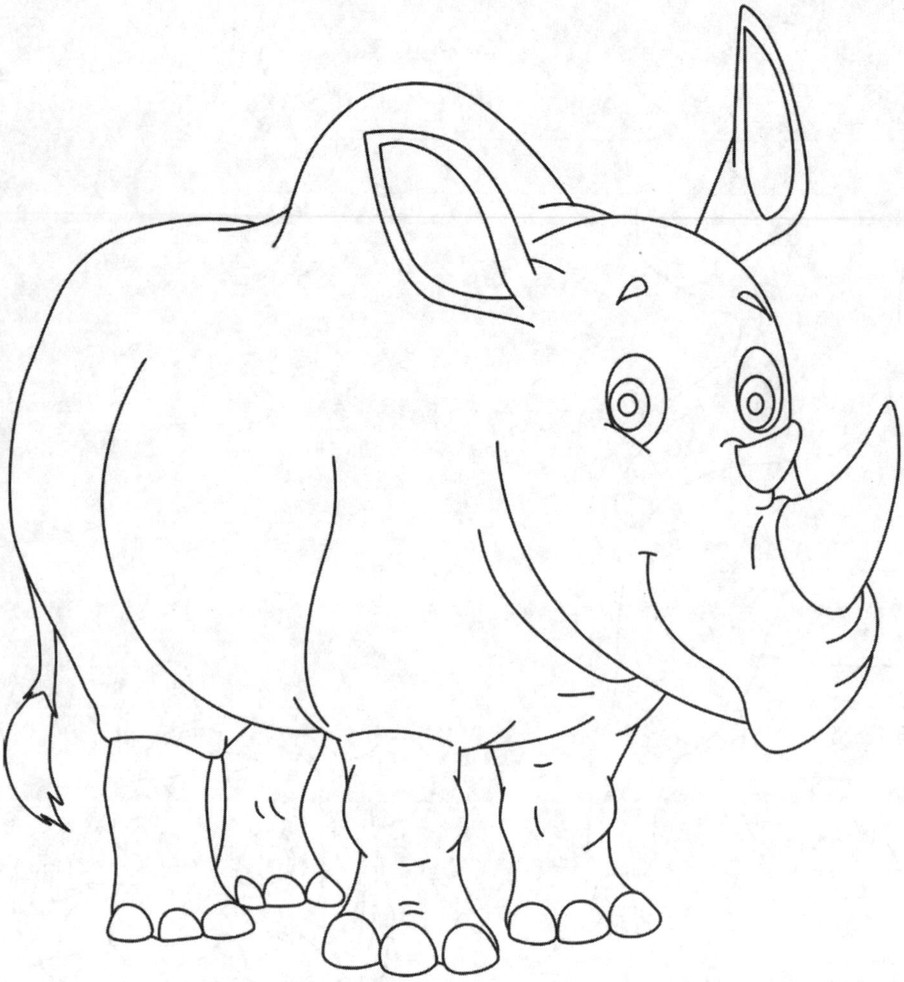

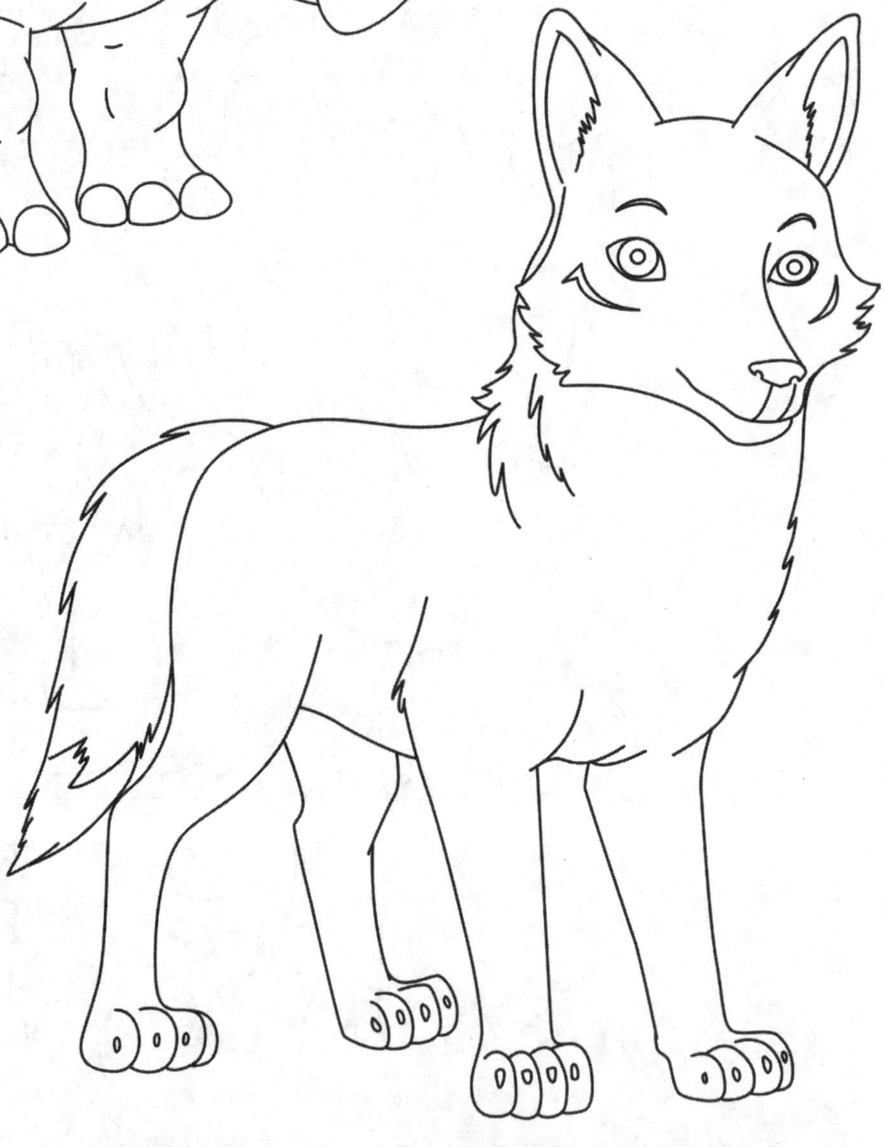

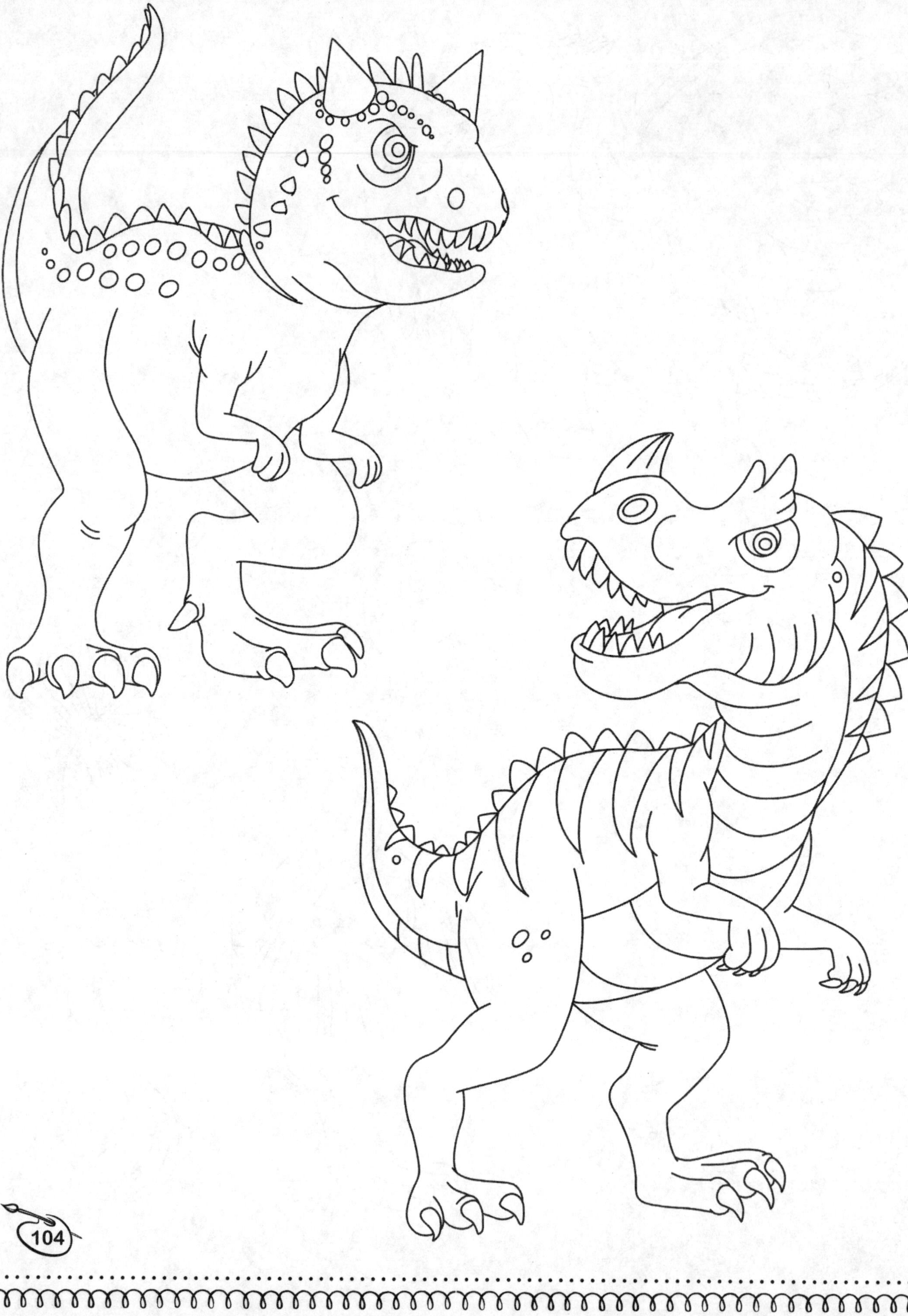

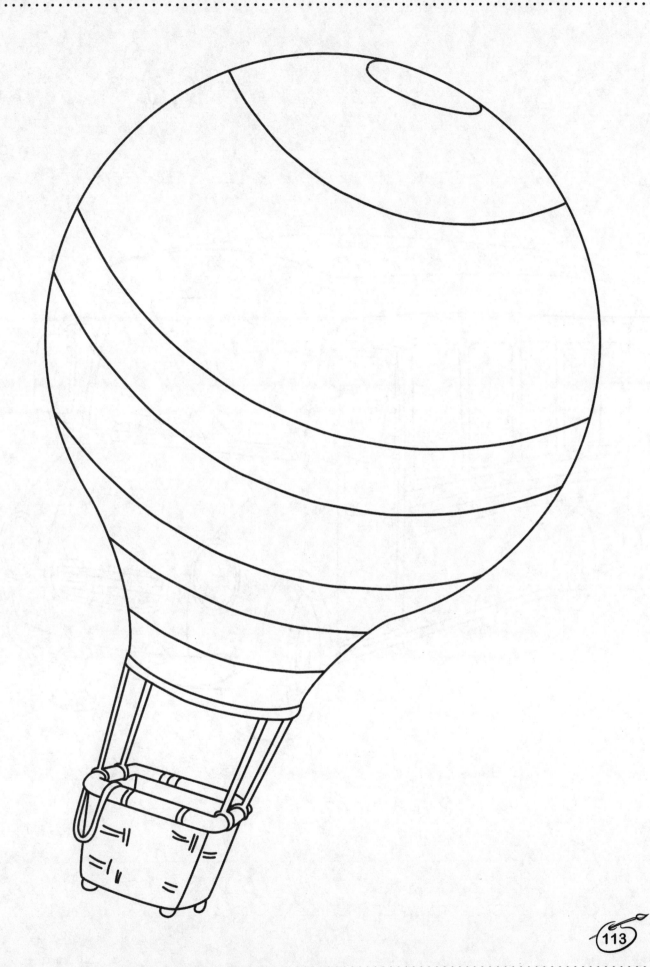

SCHOOL BUS

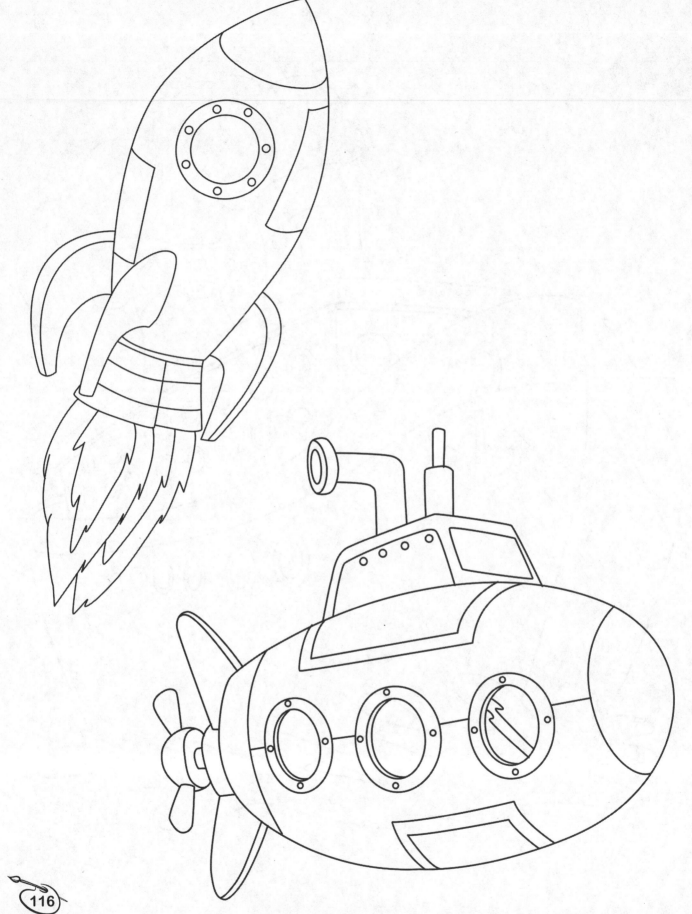

119

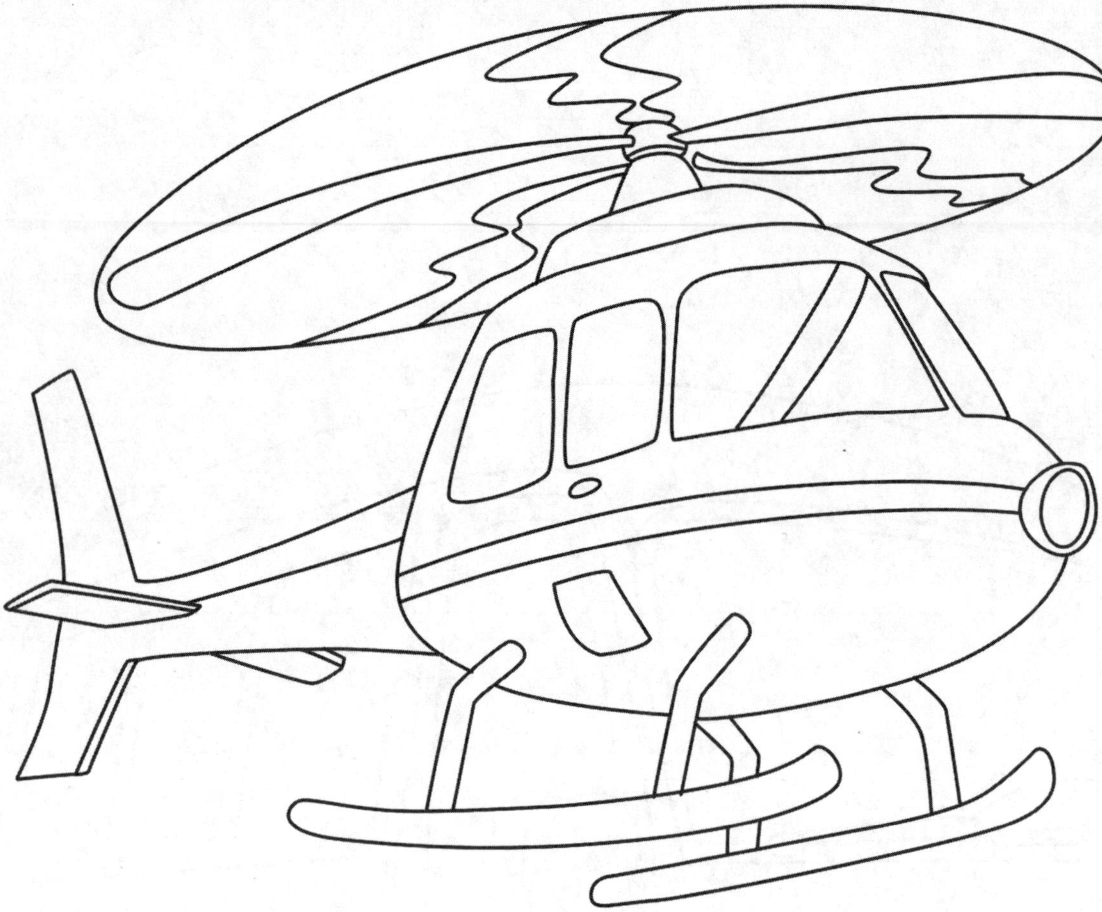

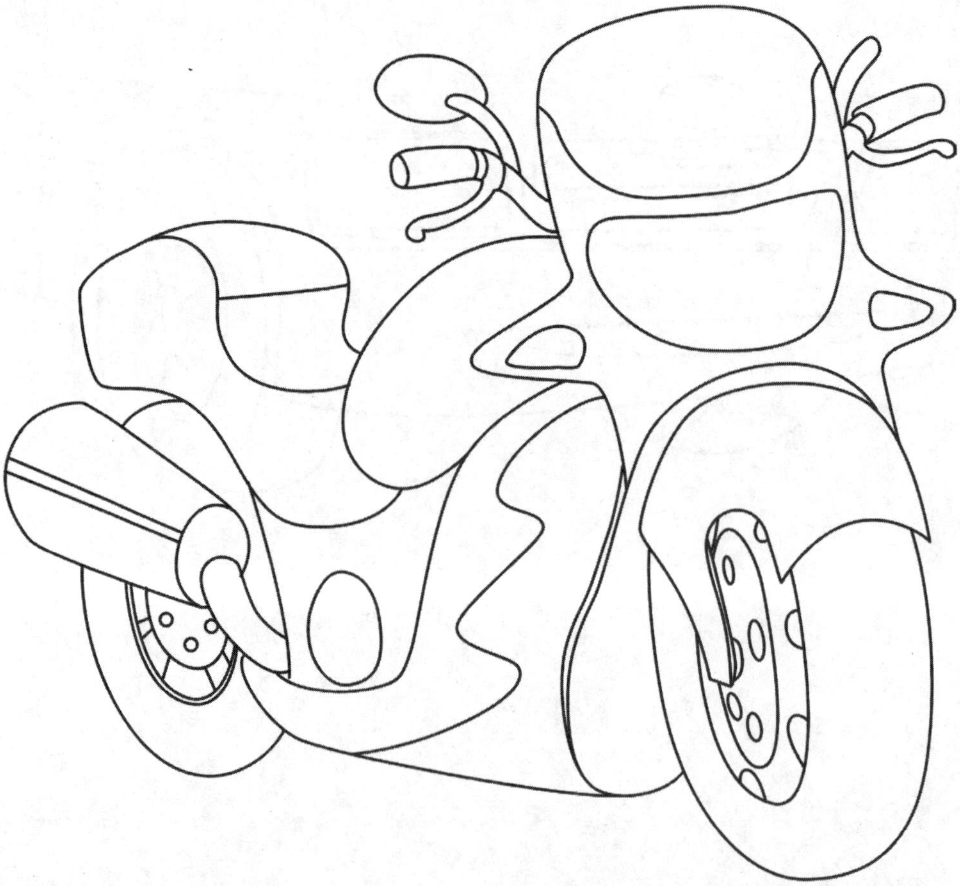

133

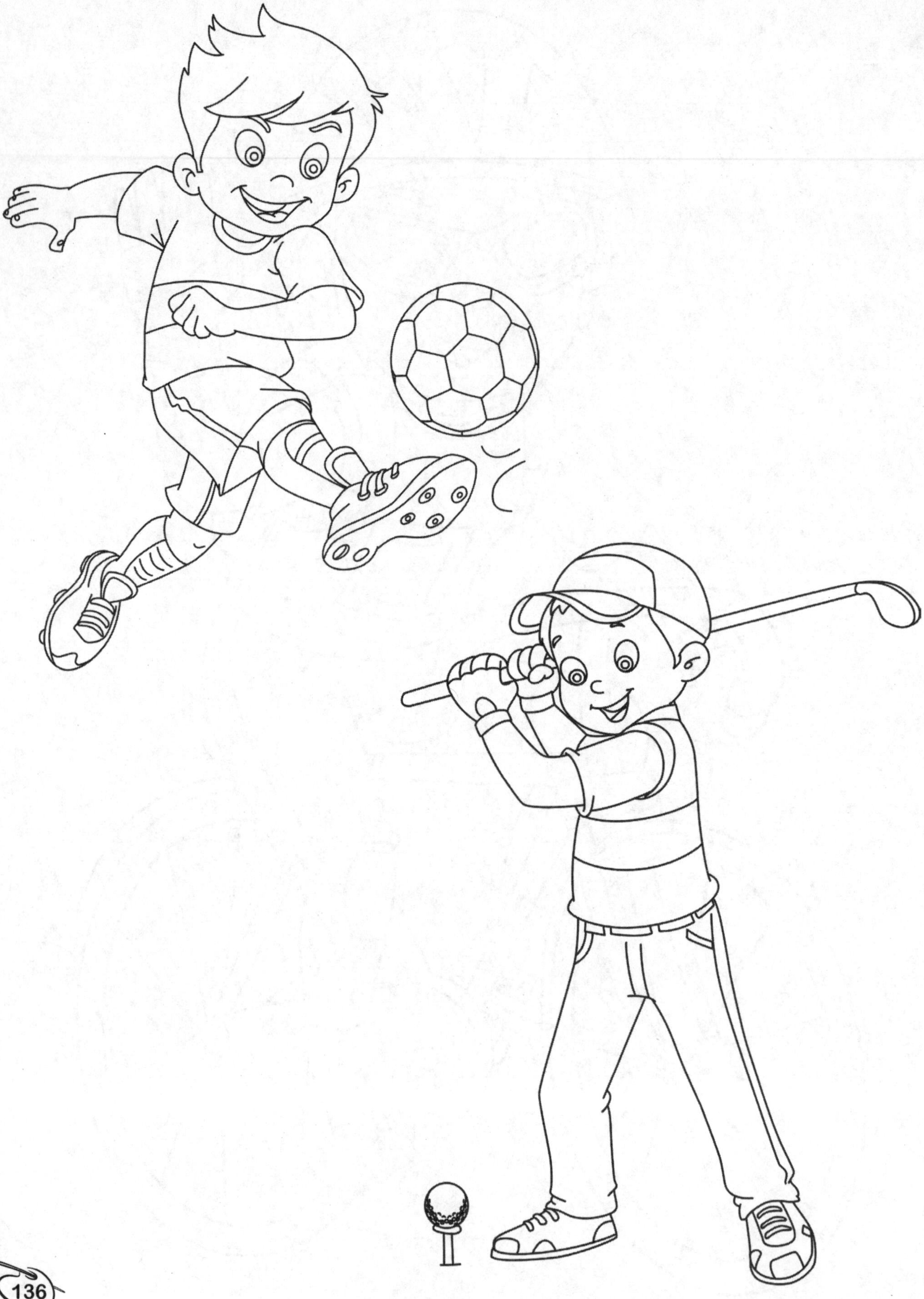

138

140

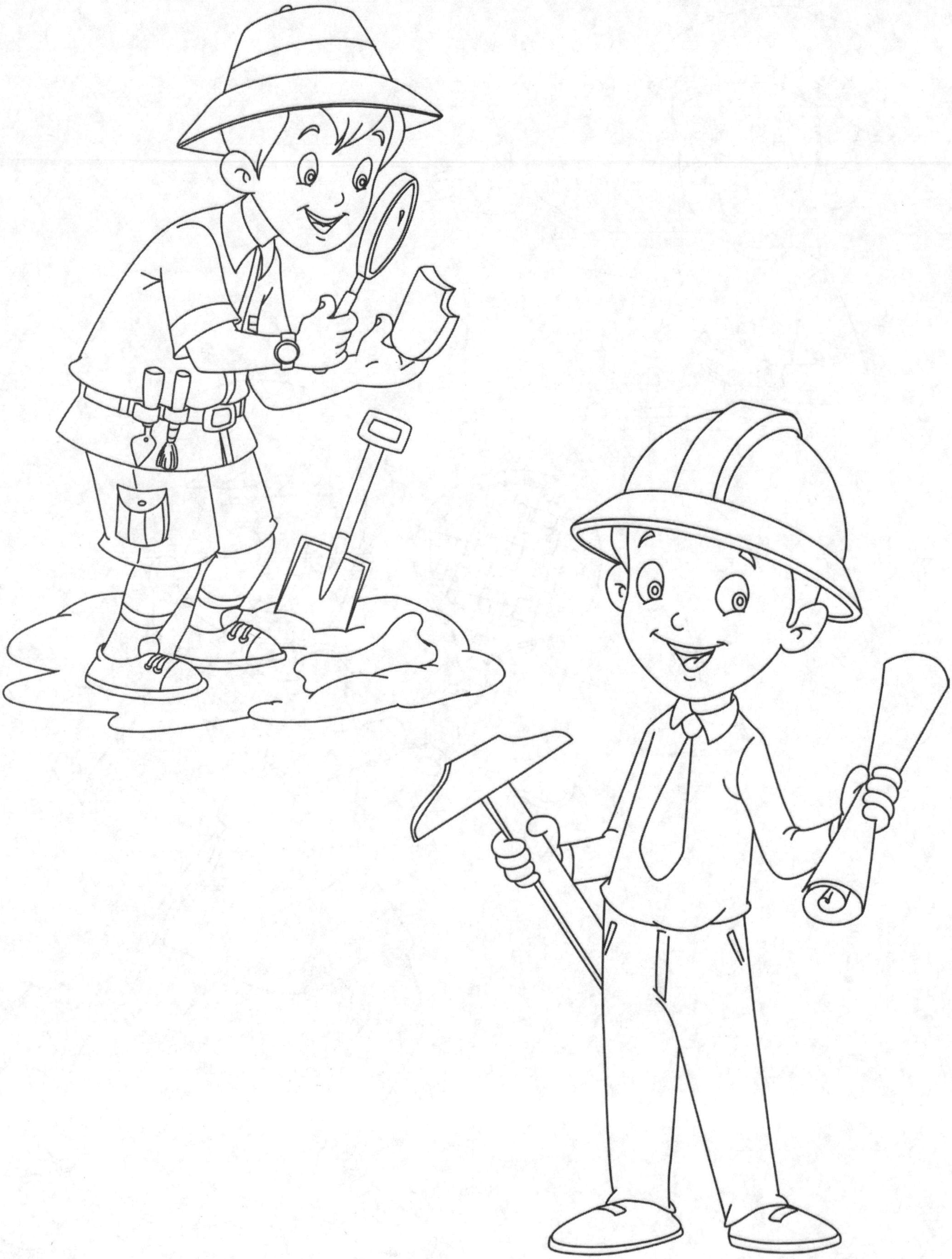

143

153

155

158

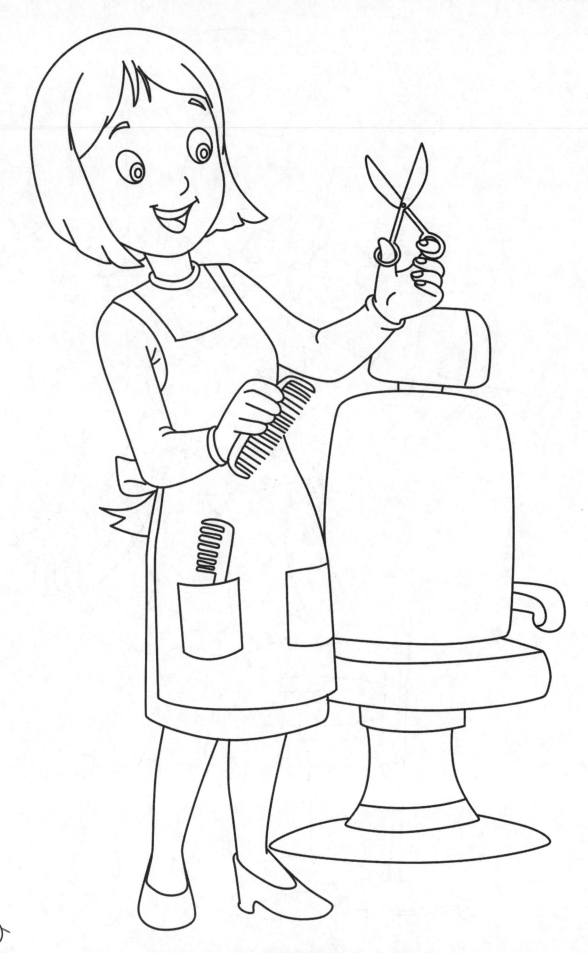

161

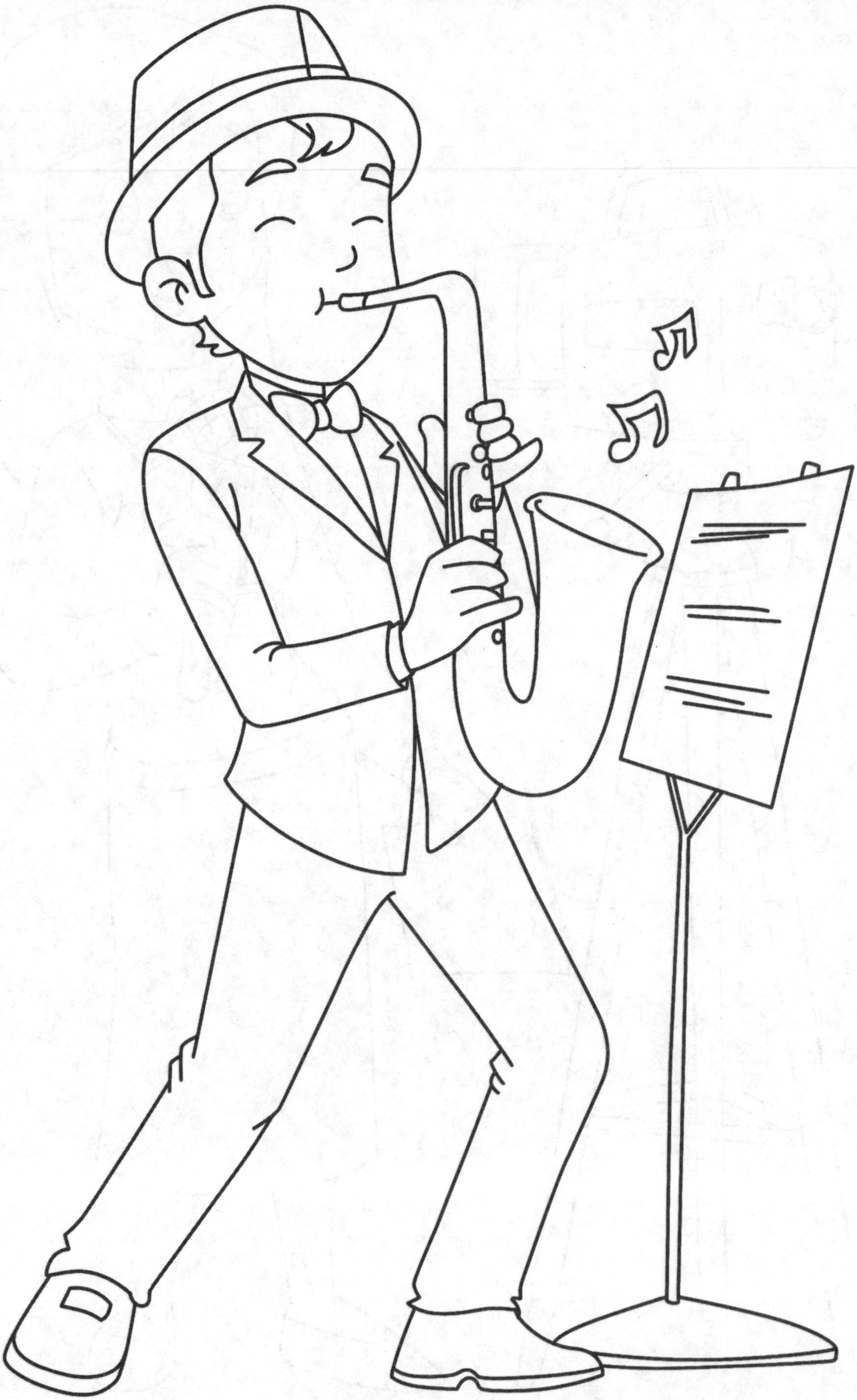

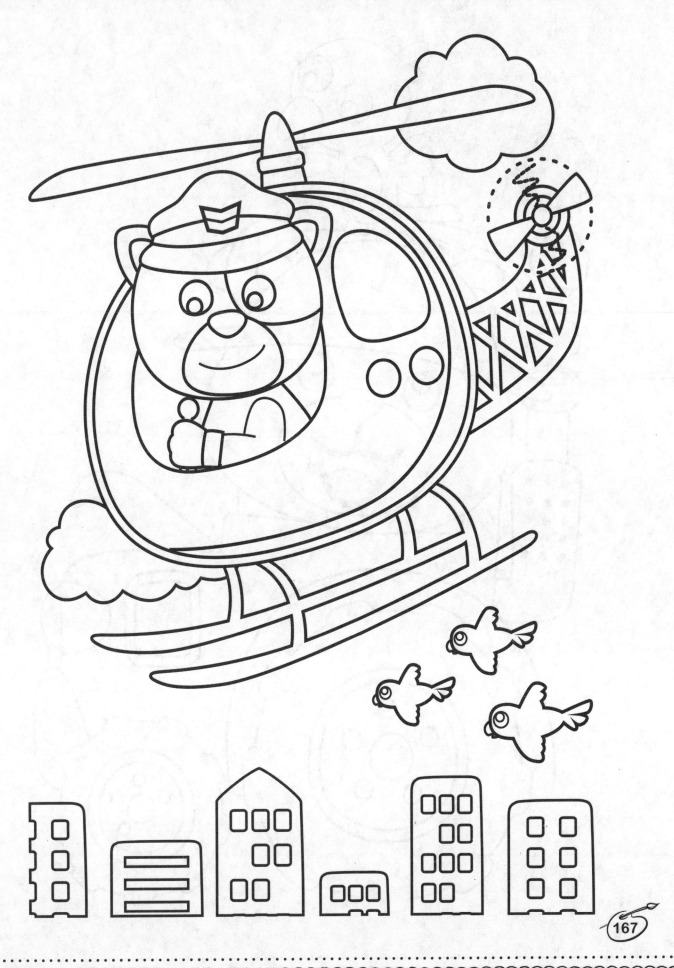

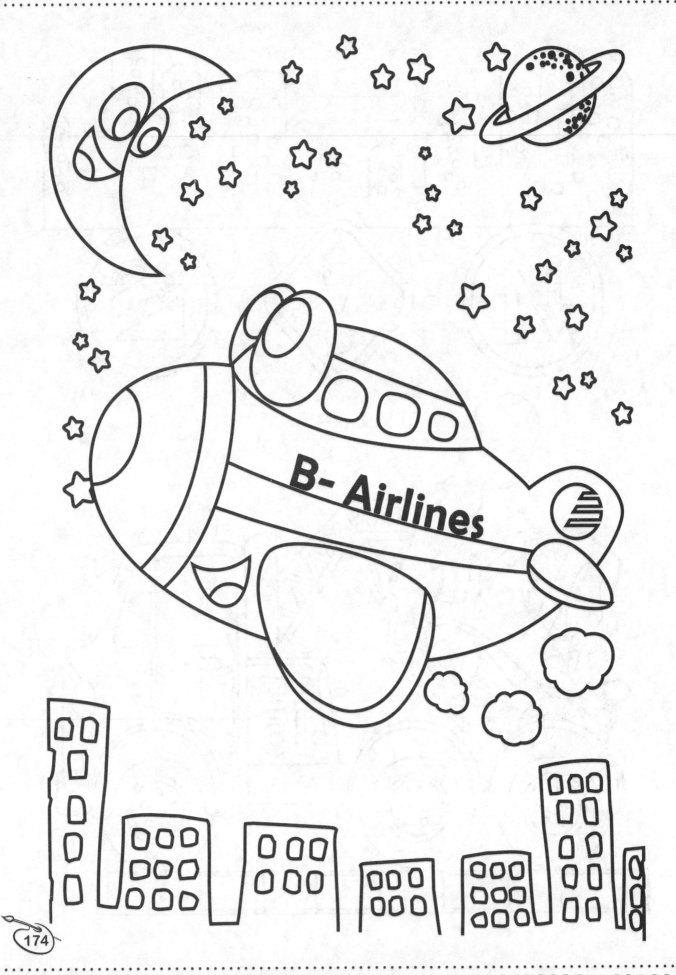

B- Airlines

174

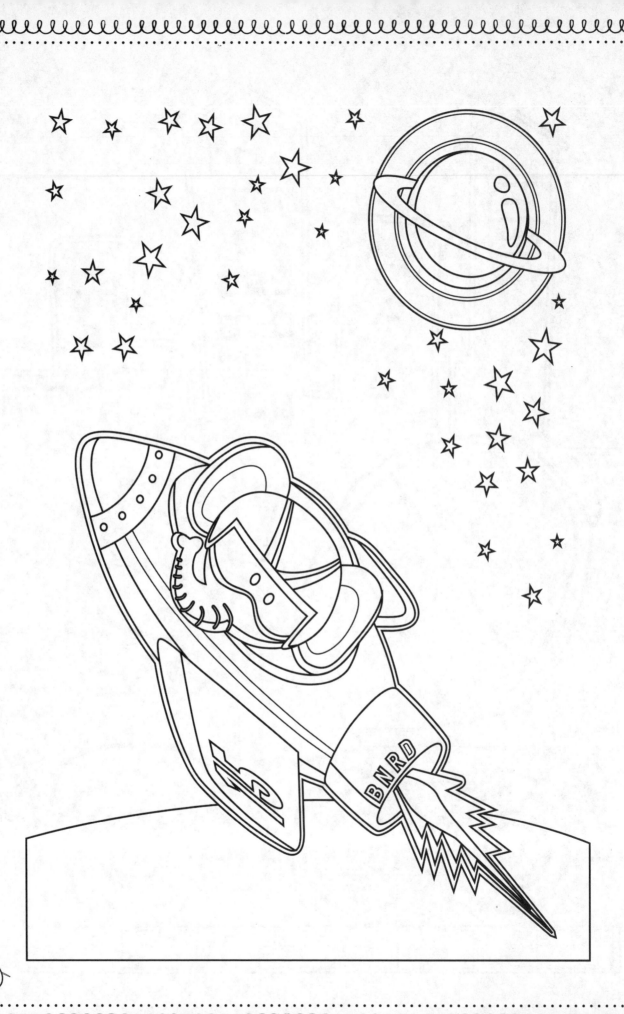

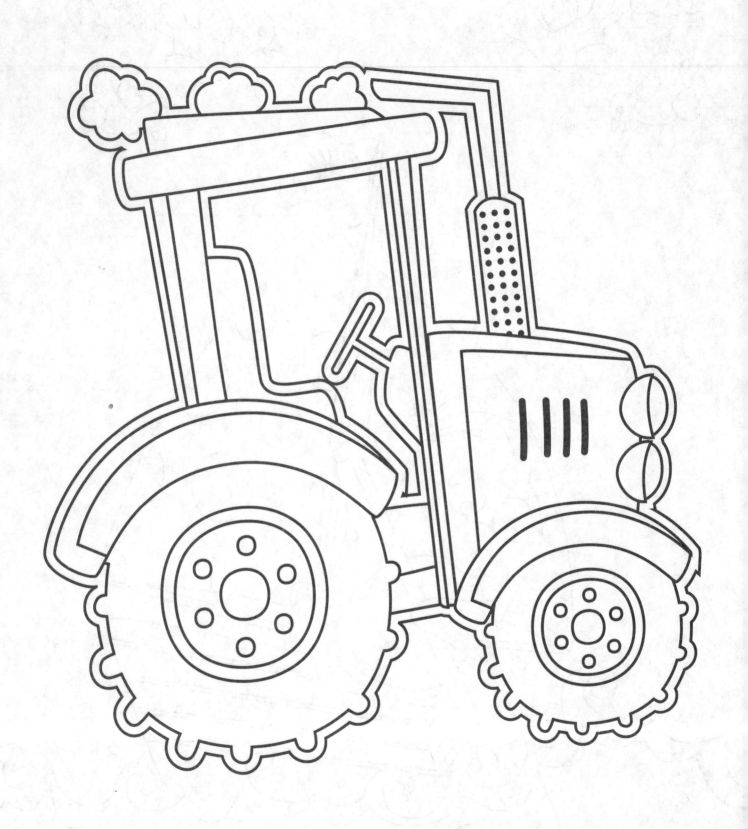

193

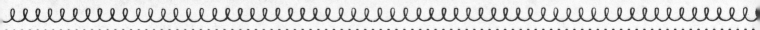

203

205

207

214

215

230

233

239

240

241

252

253

255